HEARTBEATS
and Other Stories

HEARTBEATS

and Other Stories

by Peter D. Sieruta

1817

HARPER & ROW, PUBLISHERS
Grand Rapids, Philadelphia, St. Louis, San Francisco, London, Singapore,
Sydney, Tokyo
NEW YORK

Typography by Joyce Hopkins
2 3 4 5 6 7 8 9 10

Library of Congress Cataloging-in-Publication Data
Sieruta, Peter D.
    Heartbeats and other stories / Peter D. Sieruta.
        p.   cm.
    Summary: Includes nine short stories covering such themes as sibling rivalry,
friendship, a room of one's own, madness, first love, and lost love.
    ISBN 0-06-025848-9 : $.   ISBN 0-06-025849-7 (lib. bdg.) : $
    1. Short stories, American. [1. Short stories. 2. Conduct of life—Fiction.] I.
Title.
PZ7.S5774He 1989   88-21351
[Fic]—dc19   CIP
                                                                    AC

To John and Juanita Sieruta
for *more* than 25 good reasons
and with at least a million thank yous

Contents

25 Good Reasons for Hating My Brother Todd

Give me a pencil and a piece of paper and I'll start to make a list. That's just the way I am. My brother thinks it's dumb.

1. My brother thinks most of the things I do are dumb.

But I don't care. Lists are the only way to get life into order. Can I help it if I like being organized?

2. My brother thinks I'm too organized.

"You're too uptight, kid," Todd told me tonight at dinner. "You gotta loosen up, mellow out, go with the flow."

I chewed my pork chop slowly, trying to think of the ultimate putdown that would make him clutch his heart and gasp for air. But by the time I swallowed, I still hadn't thought of it. So I just said, "Do you have any suggestions?"

"The briefcase has *got* to go," he said. "*Nobody* at school carries a briefcase."

"Mr. Samuels does."

"He's the principal! The principal can get away with it! A tenth grader can't."

"I like to keep my papers in order."

"And those glasses, they're ancient history! Nobody wears that kind anymore. Not to mention your clothes."

"What's wrong with my clothes?" I asked.

"What's *right* with them?"

"I think your brother dresses very nicely," said my mother. "He dresses like he takes school seriously. You don't see him in jeans and a T-shirt."

"That's what I mean," said Todd. "Of *course* you like how he dresses. He dresses like *Dad*."

"What's wrong with the way I dress?" my father asked.

"Nothing, but you're old. Emery shouldn't dress like a *forty-year-old*, for God's sake!"

"Please don't take the Lord's name in vain," said my mother.

"Forget it then! Forget it! Let him act like he's forty years old!" Todd shouted, gesturing wildly. "I thought I was doing him a favor. At school they're calling him *nerd*, Mom! And everyone knows he's my brother!" He stormed out of the room.

3. My brother is ashamed of me.

I folded my napkin and placed it beside my plate. "I've never heard anyone at school call me a nerd,"

I said. This wasn't quite true, but I thought it made me look a little better in their eyes. Who wants a son that people call nerd?

"Of course they don't," said my mother.

"And nobody says anything about my clothes, or my glasses or my briefcase either."

"Of course they don't," said my father.

"May I be excused?" I asked.

I didn't hear the answer because right then Todd's stereo broke the sound barrier. He always sets the volume at 10+, and his favorite music is punk rock.

4. He has no consideration for others.

5. He has rotten taste in music.

My mother cupped her hands to her mouth and yelled, "Don't worry, he'll be leaving soon. He's supposed to pick up his date at seven thirty."

I had to go to the bathroom, but when I got to the top of the stairs I saw the bathroom door was closed and heard the shower running.

6. He always hogs the bathroom.

I pounded on the door. "Hurry up. I have to go to the bathroom."

"What?"

"Hurry up, I have to go to the bathroom."

"What?"

Then he suddenly turned the shower off while I continued yelling, and the whole neighborhood probably heard me shout, "I have to go to the bathroom!"

7. Often, he deliberately embarrasses me.

3

He said, "Well come on in and use it then, you idiot."

"With you in there?" I said. "Forget it."

The shower started up again. "It's your bladder," he yelled.

8. He is disgusting!

I went into my room, shut the door, and started making a list of twenty-five ways to kill my brother. Wire his bed with dynamite? Put a rattlesnake in his closet? A couple seconds later he came in without knocking.

9. He has no respect for my privacy.

He padded across the room in his underwear. "I need socks," he said, pulling open my drawer.

10. He has no respect for my property.

"Leave my socks alone," I said.

"Oh come on, little bro," he said, trying on my only-worn-once brown argyles. "I need 'em for my date." He danced around my room. "Now I've got socks appeal!"

11. My brother has a very, very bad sense of humor.

"Just get the hell out of my room," I said. I could feel my face getting red—and all because he'd mentioned the date out loud.

He put on his mock shocked look and clapped his hands to the sides of his face. "Oh, Mom," he yelled. "Emery said the *h* word!"

12. He's always trying to get me in trouble.

"I mean it, Todd, leave me alone. Go on your stupid date and leave me alone!"

"All right, all right, I'm going," he said. Then he mooned me.

"You're sick," I said, throwing a notebook at him.

He ran out of my room laughing, and I returned to my list of ways to kill him. Put insect repellent in his milk? Disconnect the brakes on his ten-speed? But none of my ideas seemed cruel enough. I crumpled the paper and tossed it toward the wastepaper basket. Of course it landed on the floor.

13. My brother has never missed a shot in wastepaper basketball.

Why did he have to mention the stupid date, anyway? Was he just trying to see my reaction? Well, forget it! I wasn't about to give him the satisfaction. I pulled out another notebook and started working on my science project, but I couldn't stop myself from going over the last couple days in my mind. Because it was the science project that had started the whole thing.

Let me make one thing perfectly clear: I hate group projects, team projects, class projects, et cetera. In other words, anything that means I can't work alone. Frankly, there's nobody in my classes that I care to work with. Even more frankly: There's nobody that cares to work with me. So when Mr. Jamison said we'd have to pair off for our final science project, I didn't exactly jump for joy. Usually everyone teamed with their friends and I was one of the leftovers, destined to be paired off with some other loser by the teacher—a situation that had, in the past, made me partners with an illiterate girl, our class dope pusher, and a Swedish exchange student who could only say "yah." But this time Mr. Jamison said that partners were going to be assigned.

As he read through the list, accompanied by cheers and groans from the class, I read the next chapter in the textbook. It really didn't matter whom I was paired with—I'd probably end up doing all the work. Just then I heard my name. "Emery, you and Jodi Meriwether will be working together."

Everyone started laughing, and I turned to look at Jodi just in time to see her making barfing faces at the girl sitting next to her. I had to turn away, because Jodi was just too lovely to look at for more than a second. Ever since fourth grade I've wanted to marry Jodi Meriwether. She is, without a single doubt, the most beautiful, popular, poised teenage person ever to attend Truman High. I knew she wasn't too crazy about me, but then, we'd never really gotten to know each other very well.

For the rest of the class period I calmly copied lecture notes, while in a corner of my mind I had visions of Jodi and myself accepting our Nobel Prize in Chemistry. I also had other visions of us, but they were X rated.

The bell rang and I jumped out of my seat. Usually it takes Jodi a long time to leave the classroom. She always stops to talk to at least three or four people (never me) and sometimes even the teacher. I know, because sometimes I have trouble with the lock on my briefcase and it takes me a long time to leave too. But that day the bell hadn't even finished ringing before Jodi was out of her seat and running toward the door. She was fumbling with her books, trying to shove her papers into a binder. I got to the doorway just in time to see her books crash to the floor.

I knelt down to help her, saying, "When should we start working on the project?"

"Don't mention that project!" she snapped.

"How about today—this afternoon?"

"No. Would you get away from me!"

"We're going to have to start someday," I said, then swallowed the heartbeat in my throat and added, "Jodi."

"What?"

"What what?" I said.

"You said my name."

"I said that we're going to have to start some-day . . . Jodi."

People were coming out of the room, making sarcastic remarks about Jodi and me on the floor together. Jodi looked like she wanted to bite someone.

"Can't we start today?" I asked. "At my house?"

She looked past me at all the other people streaming into the hallway and hissed, "Yesss, okay, all right, now just *get out of here*!"

I didn't think that was a very gracious thing to say,

but I handed her my address and went on to my next class.

On the way home from school I ran into the corner store for a snack to serve when Jodi came over, though I wasn't sure what to buy. Todd would probably pick up a bag of Doritos, but I rejected that as too common. I also rejected pizza rolls (too messy) and cupcakes (too sticky). So I ended up buying Doritos anyway, though they turned out to be a complete waste because when I got home I accidentally dropped my briefcase on top of them and smashed the whole bag.

I was right back where I started from, and the only things in the refrigerator were a pot roast and some vegetables. I raced back and forth, finding a pot and cutting up potatoes, and almost had the roast in the oven when I realized something: Pot roast is not your typical after-school snack. Okay, Emery, *calm down*, I told myself. Everything's going to be all right. I sat down and began making a list of all the things we could talk about (the weather, classes, the science project). Then I began pacing, running to the window every five seconds and not acting like myself at all.

When the doorbell rang, I tripped over a throw rug and hit the door with my head. "What was that thud?" was the first thing Jodi said after I opened the door.

"What thud?" I said, pressing my hand against my forehead and praying there wouldn't be a lump.

I had planned to say "Jodi, Jodi, Jodi" when I opened the door, because that's the kind of thing Todd's always saying to girls, but the thud had destroyed the moment.

It was almost like a dream come true to see Jodi standing in the middle of our living room, slowly unwinding her long orange scarf. "Isn't your mother or somebody here?" she asked, looking around.

"Are you afraid to be alone with me?" I asked.

"You've *got* to be kidding," she snorted.

"I was thinking, maybe, the kitchen . . . we could study there." My words were coming out all mixed up, and it was all Jodi's fault for looking the way she did. Nobody should look that good, except maybe Miss America or a TV star. Jodi was wearing a purple sweater and jeans. They were both very tight.

She followed me into the kitchen, and I turned on the light over the table. "I had some Doritos, but I dropped my briefcase on them." I hadn't meant to say that, but I was really stumped for a conversation opener.

Jodi snorted.

"How do you feel about pot roast?"

"I'm on a diet. Now, about this science project—"

"A diet? Jodi, no. You don't need to diet. You're perfect. Your figure, I mean." I could feel my face turning hot, so finished up with a lame: "I mean, you're not fat."

She said, "About this science project. I know you're supposed to be this big brain and everything, but really, science just isn't my thing. So I was thinking, my older brother's got this solar-system thing he made about five years ago out of coat hangers and spray-painted Styrofoam balls. What if I just brought that over as *my* contribution and then *you* could write up some kind of really complicated paper about it and we could turn it in? I'm not into science."

"A brain?" I said. "You think I'm a brain?" That clinched it. I was in love.

"So what do you think?" she asked, getting up from her chair as if the whole discussion were over. The light glowed on her long blond hair.

"About what?"

"The Styrofoam solar system! Aren't you listening to me?"

"Of course I'm listening." I paused for a second, thinking: *A Styrofoam solar system?* How do you tell the girl you love that her suggestion is the pits?

I straightened my glasses and cleared my throat. "Sit down, Jodi," I said in a calm voice. She looked a little bewildered, but she did sit down. "Solar systems are good—very good—for science projects, but you have to remember this is *tenth* grade. I think maybe we should try for something a little more challenging."

"My cousin's got a plaster-of-paris volcano I could probably borrow," she said.

"Maybe something even more challenging than that," I said.

"It really erupts, too."

"What would you say if I told you we might be capable—you and I—of turning in the best science project ever at that school? I think we could do it."

"The best?" she asked, her eyes widening. Because if there was one thing Jodi was interested in, it was being the best.

I leaned in closer and looked her right in the eyes. "The best *ever*," I said, opening my notebook. "I made a list of some concepts in study hall." And there they were—twenty-five individual suggestions—not just ideas, but real concepts with pros and cons and costs and conclusions and everything. Jodi pulled the notebook toward her and began reading through the list. I loved the way her lips moved slightly as she read but pushed that thought from my mind; now wasn't the time to think about love. First I should win her respect and admiration. Love was sure to follow.

Just then I heard the front door open. "Anybody home?" yelled Todd. "Mama Bear? Papa Bear? Emery Bear?"

14. He can't even walk in the front door without making a big deal out of it.

"Who's that?" asked Jodi, looking up from the notebook.

I said, "Keep reading."

Todd appeared in the kitchen doorway wearing his soccer uniform and bouncing a soccer ball off his biceps.

15. He has biceps. Big ones.

"Hi," he said.

Jodi looked up, and a slow smile spread across her face. "Hi!" she said.

"We're working," I told Todd sternly.

"Okay. See you later. I've got to shower." He turned and walked down the hall. Jodi and I were both watching him. When he got out of sight, he said, "By the way, who's the beautiful girl sitting at our kitchen table?"

Jodi burst out laughing as if that were the wittiest remark she had ever heard. "I'm Jodi Meriwether," she called.

We could hear his footsteps going up the stairs. "Glad to know you, Jodi."

Jodi turned back to look at me with a stunned smile on her face. "Wow," was all she said.

"Back to these concepts—" I said.

"Was that your *brother*?" she gasped.

"Him? Oh, yeah, I guess it was."

"Your brother? How can it be?"

"Well, let's see, project thirteen right here is all about genetics. Maybe if we work on that you'll get a better understa—"

"Is he *adopted* or something?" she asked. She was looking at me more intensely than she had all afternoon.

"No. And neither am I."

"But he's so . . . so . . . blond!"

"So what?" I said. My mother has blond hair, my

father has blond hair, all my grandparents have or had blond hair. My hair is dark. Very dark. People are always asking us what color hair our milkman has. I don't find this funny. Neither do my parents. My brother finds it hilarious.

"He's like . . . like . . . a Norse god!"

"Jodi, have you ever actually *seen* a Norse god?"

16. He's six feet tall.

17. He has green eyes.

18. He has teeth like Chiclets.

19. He looks great in a soccer uniform.

"Does your brother go to another school or something, Emery?" It was the first time she ever said my name out loud.

"No, he goes to Truman too."

"What! I've never seen him around!"

"Well, you know how it is. He's a senior, and—"

Jodi grabbed onto the edge of the kitchen table. "A senior?" she shrieked.

"We won't get to be *juniors* if we don't pass this science class," I said, trying to turn the conversation back to where I could handle it.

She looked down at the notebook in front of her as if she'd forgotten its existence. "Oh, that's right," she said.

"Look, maybe a Styrofoam solar system is the way to go," I said.

"Oh, no. No, Emery. I think we should do the *greatest* project ever in the history of the school."

"Really?"

"Absolutely. We could work on it every after-noon, over here."

"Which concept are you interested in?" I asked.

"Um . . . eight," she said, pointing at the note-book.

The shower stopped running. Todd yelled down the stairs, "Hey, who wants to help dry my back?"

Jodi actually jumped up!

I grabbed her wrist. She looked embarrassed. I pretended not to notice. She said, "Not too cool." I could feel little sparks of electricity dancing up and down my arm. My hand was still around her wrist as she sat down again. The electric sparks had turned to jolts. I looked at her face, but all I could see was her embarrassment for jumping up like that. I let go.

She looked down at the Formica tabletop. After a second she said, "God. Embarrassment. I'm not usu-ally like this."

"It's all right, Jodi," I said.

She looked at me then. Her eyes were partly hid-den by her hair, but a slow smile began to appear. I wanted to hug her. "You know, I've misjudged you. I used to think you were a nerd, like everyone says, but really, you're not."

"Thanks."

"I mean that. You're different than I thought. You're okay, Emery."

"Thanks." What did this mean? I didn't want to get my hopes up.

14

Jodi continued: "And I'm really looking forward to this project. I know we'll do a good job, with you being such a brain and everything. I really mean it. I'm not saying that because of . . . him."

"What's up, guys?" Todd was standing in the doorway. He had changed clothes, and his hair was still wet.

"We're working on a science project together," said Jodi. She was still blushing, but it just made her look even prettier.

"Oh," he said, pouring some orange juice. "Then you've got yourself a great partner, Jodi. This kid's a brain."

"I know!" she said.

"Oh, cut it out," I said modestly.

"And he's so *organized*," said Jodi. "You should see this list."

"Oh, I've *seen* his lists." Todd sat down at the table and said, "Emer—ee—ee—ee—ee—ee—ee—ee," giving the back of my hair a tug with each "ee." He does that all the time and he knows it drives me crazy.

"Stop it," I said.

Jodi was laughing. So was Todd.

He tilted his chair back until the front legs rose off the floor. Just one little push backward, I thought. . . . But instead I held my hands very tightly together and watched while Todd hung perfectly balanced in the air, taking a long, long swallow of juice.

20. He's a show-off.

Then he brought the chair back down and said, "Science projects, huh? I remember them well. I had Jamison for tenth-grade science."

"Me too!" shrieked Jodi. "He's our teacher! What a coincidence!"

"Old Blue Hands," said Todd, then started to laugh.

"Blue hands? *What!*" said Jodi, laughing too. She was leaning halfway across the table.

"Jamison used to have blue hands—no joke! We were doing this experiment, making crystals on charcoal briquets, and he accidentally spilled the solution all over the lab table and tried to clean it up with some Kleenex, and he ended up with bright blue hands. And it wouldn't come off. He had blue hands for the whole semester!"

Jodi was laughing hysterically.

Todd was laughing so hard at his own story that he was pounding his fist on the table.

21. He always laughs at his own jokes.

"Well, he *deserved* the blue hands, for God's sake," said Todd, wiping at his eyes. "That's what he gets for doing those dumb first-grade type of experiments. I mean, we used to make crystals on charcoal in *grade* school, right, Em?"

"I don't recall."

"Well, what kind of experiments would *you* suggest for a tenth-grade class?" said Jodi.

"Transplants!" shouted Todd, pounding the table again. "And test-tube babies!"

"Oh, for goodness' sakes, Todd. We're trying to study."

"Can't you just see it, Todd?" said Jodi. "Hey, Mr. Jamison, come look in my test tube. I think it's *breathing!*"

"My test tube's having twins!" said Todd, then: "Where are you going?"

"To get my briefcase, if that's okay with you two!" I stomped into the living room, grabbed the case, then stomped back into the kitchen. "Since I don't think we'll be doing much more work on this today, I'm going to put away all these notes," I said to Jodi.

"Oh, Emery, don't be so . . . so . . ." she said. "Come on, sit down, we can work on it in a while."

I sat down because I wanted to please Jodi. But as I listened to them talk and laugh, I knew I was watching my beloved, my sweetness, my life, slowly ebb away.

And I knew damn well whose fault it was.

Later, after Jodi left, Todd came into my room and sat on my bed, messing up the fresh sheets as he bounced around. "So how goes it, little bro?" he asked.

"I'm trying to study."

"It kills me," he said. "Here you are, straight-A brain, you don't even *need* to study, but you do it

17

all the time. Then there's me, dummo jock who *should* study all the time, and I *never* do."

"You do okay."

"*Okay*, yeah, but not all A's like you."

He was trying to get on my good side.

"What do you want from me?"

"Can't you trust me, for God's sake? Can't I even give you a compliment? Do you always think I've got an ulterior motive?"

I turned and stared at him. Finally I nodded. He laughed, then looked up at me sheepishly. "Okay, you're right. There *is* an ulterior motive. Would it be okay with you if I asked Jodi for a date?"

I knew it! But still . . . hearing it out loud was something else. It hurt.

I looked at the wall in front of my desk. It was very white. "Sure," I said. "Why are you asking *me*, anyway? We don't have anything going."

"I know. But she is your friend and all, so I wouldn't feel right about it if you had objections."

"No objections," I said.

"She's pretty neat, huh?"

"I guess."

"Pretty neat looking. And I like the way she laughs."

"She laughs okay, if you like laughing."

"*Like* laughing? I *love* laughing!" He bounced up and down on my bed a few more times.

Suddenly I jumped up and shouted, "Would you

18

stop doing that, please? Would you stop bouncing on my bed?"

He stopped. He just sat there in the middle of the bed, staring at me in surprise.

I gripped the back of my chair as hard as I could. "Maybe you should have a little consideration for other people once in a while instead of jumping on their beds all the time!" I shouted. "I wish you'd grow up. You're supposed to be the older brother, after all. But no! You're always running all over the place, waving your arms around, talking in italics. You make me mad, Todd!"

"Talking in *italics*?" he said. "What are you talking about?"

"There! You just did it there. You said, 'Talking in *italics*?' If you were in a book, half the things you'd say would be in italics!"

"I don't get it, Emery."

"Of course you don't. You don't get *anything*!" That's how far he'd driven me. Now even *I* was talking in italics.

"Does this have anything to do with Jodi?"

Suddenly I was tired. I sat down at my desk and laid my head in my arms. When I spoke, my voice sounded weak. "Of course it doesn't have anything to do with Jodi. Go ahead, take her out, she's nice."

"You feeling okay, Em?" He sounded concerned. I hate being pitied.

I tried to turn it into a joke and said, "I'm just tired.

It's not easy being a ner—" The word broke in half as it came out of my mouth. "—erd."

"You're not . . . crying, are you?"

"No! Why would I be?" I lifted my head and took off my glasses to prove my eyes were completely dry.

Then I dropped my head back on the desk and shut my eyes. I could still feel Todd standing right behind the chair. He lightly punched me in the shoulder a couple of times. Then he took his fist and rubbed it up and down my back for a second. I really did start to cry at this point, but very quietly, so he couldn't tell. In fact, he probably thought I'd fallen asleep, because shortly after that he tiptoed from the room.

That was last night, and tonight was The Date. Of course she said yes when he called her.

22. Girls always say yes to Todd.

As I sat in my room, I could hear him downstairs, talking to my parents.

"Emery! Emery!" my mother called. "Bring your camera down and take a picture of Todd."

"Mother, for goodness' sakes, why?" I asked, but brought the camera downstairs anyway. "It's not as if he's going to his senior prom or anything. He's just going to see another horror movie with some girl."

"Yes, but I'd like to have a reminder that at some point in his adolescence, Todd got dressed up in

20

something other than jeans or a soccer uniform."

I said, "Don't you usually just wear jeans and a T-shirt on a date anyway?"

"Yeah, but this isn't just any date. *You* know. Jodi's pretty special. She doesn't seem like the jeans type." I wondered what Jodi would wear.

"Should I take the picture or shouldn't I?" I asked. "I've got more important things to do."

"Take the picture," my mother said firmly.

Todd stood in front of the curtains and raised his eyebrows and smiled at me, as if he hated getting his picture taken but was just humoring our mother.

23. He loves getting his picture taken.

I snapped the picture, making sure that my thumb was in front of the lens.

"Let's take another one, just in case the first one doesn't come out or something," he said.

"Sure," I said, taking another picture of my thumb.

He grabbed his car keys and said, "Who knows what the night holds? Movies, dinner, dancing?" He grabbed my mother and twirled her through a few dance steps.

"You're just going to some dumb horror movie. You've already eaten, so you're not going to dinner. And you're not going dancing . . . are you?" The thought of Todd holding Jodi in his arms was too much to take.

"Don't know, can't say, not sure," said Todd.

"Just be careful with the car," said my father, "and be back by midnight."

"Sure thing. I'll be back by midnight. Twelve thirty at the latest, Dad. . . . Maybe one o'clock if traffic's heavy." He ran out the door and vaulted over the hedge next to the driveway.

My father shook his head, smiled, and said, "Son of a gun."

24. *Todd always,* always *gets whatever he wants.*

The car radio suddenly began to scream at its maximum volume, and our old Pontiac went roaring down into the street.

I don't know what kept me standing at the doorway, watching the car until it went out of sight. By all rights, I should have been the one driving off to Jodi's house at that very moment . . . even if I don't know how to drive yet. I sighed and sat down in a living-room chair.

"What's the matter?" said my mother.

"Nothing."

I took out my ballpoint and wrote on the first page of this notebook, "25 Good Reasons for Hating My Brother Todd." The first thing I thought of was that my brother thinks it's dumb that I like lists. "What are you doing?" my mother asked, snooping over my shoulder.

"Making a list of all the reasons I hate Todd."

"Oh, stop that nonsense. You don't hate Todd.

What's wrong? Are you angry because he's taking out that girl from your class?"

"Angry?" I said. "Why should I care? I hate Jodi Meriwether. I never have liked her. You might say I despise her."

"Okay, okay, I'm sorry I asked."

"You should be," I muttered under my breath.

She said, "I just don't see why you have to behave so poorly toward your brother."

25. My mother always did like him best.

Room for Improvement

Mitch Dietrich was up early that Sunday, packing.

He stacked boxes of books and emptied his drawers as quietly as he could. In just a few hours his dream of a lifetime was going to come true; he didn't want a kid brother spoiling the big moment.

With thirteen children, two parents, two dogs, three cats and thirty-six tropical fish living in the same house, the Dietrich family was never big on traditions. "What do you mean?" Miriam, his year-younger sister, asked when Mitch brought it up. "*Having babies* is their tradition."

But after some thought Mitch and Miriam came up with three Dietrich traditions. First of all, each of the children had a name beginning with *m*. It was all right for the oldest, Mark and Matt and Mary and Melissa—and even for Mitch. But Miriam despised her name, and as the seven younger children came along, things got progressively worse: Milton, Marvin, Marigold, Muriel, Maude, Manfred and Millard.

The second Dietrich tradition was that the entire family had to go to Mass together on Christmas and Easter. But Miriam went to Mass every day. She said she wanted to be a nun if she couldn't get a boyfriend.

The third and best tradition was the room. There were four bedrooms in the Dietrich house: the parents' room, the boys' room, the girls' room, and *the* room. It didn't really need a special name; everyone in the Dietrich family knew what you meant when you said, "When I get the room, I'm going to stay up reading till two A.M. if I want. With the radio on. Alone!" or "I'm saving up to buy a stereo, for when I get the room."

The oldest child in the family always got the room. Melissa, its most recent inhabitant, was leaving for college that Sunday. Mitch planned to move in as soon as she walked out the front door.

"Whatcha doing?" Mitch almost dropped a handful of clothes hangers at the sound of little Millard's voice.

"Shh!" he said.

But a simple "shh" wouldn't work with a kid like Millard. Mitch just prayed Millard's voice wouldn't wake up Milton, Marvin, or Manfred, who slept in neighboring bunks. "Are you moving into Melissa's room *now*?" Millard persisted.

"Pretty soon," Mitch whispered.

"What if she doesn't leave today?"

"She'll leave."

"Then what if she comes back and says she wants her room back again?" Millard's favorite sentence opening was "what if." Mitch knew this kind of conversation could go on for hours.

"It will be *my* room. She can't make me leave."

"What if—"

"Millard!"

But at that moment Mitch heard voices from downstairs and knew Melissa was about to leave. He ran down to say good-bye. "You look like you can't wait for the room," said his older sister, holding onto a suitcase.

"I can't!"

"Well, enjoy it. You'll be surprised how fast the year goes by. Pretty soon you'll be the one leaving for college."

"I wish."

Mr. Dietrich jingled the car keys. "Ready, Melissa?"

"Ready," she said, moving toward the door.

"Ready," whispered Mitch, running upstairs to his new room.

Mitch shut the door firmly behind him, then turned around and around in his room, arms outstretched. I have never before felt this *great*, he thought. The closet echoed when he looked inside, the bare desk drawers slid out easily.

Mitch had been planning this move for a long time. A large part of his McDonald's paycheck had gone toward home furnishings: a small stereo system, some posters for the walls, a reading lamp. It seemed very important that everything in the room be *his*. All the pencils in his pencil holder were brand-new from Woolworth's. He stood sharpening them to razor point, loving every twist of his new nineteen-cent sharpener.

After he had shelved his books and hung his posters, Mitch ran to the store. He bought an eight-pack of Snickers, and mumbling into his collar, he asked for the September issue of *Playboy*. With four little brothers around, he never could have kept those items hidden in the boys' room. But now he had his own room—a room his mother had promised never to enter, not even to dust. Now he had his own room. . . .

When he approached the house, he saw three of the little brothers and two of the little sisters having a mud fight on the front lawn. Miriam was sitting on the porch like a thick stone statue. "You shouldn't have left the kids here alone. You were nominally in charge. . . . Do you know what 'nominally' means?" Miriam liked showing off her vocabulary.

"It means the kids would do whatever they want whether I was here or not," said Mitch.

"Where *were* you?" she persisted.

"Out." He crushed the paper bag tightly under his arm.

"Don't think that just because you've got that room for yourself you can use a deprecatory tone with me!" she said, then leaned forward, pointing. "What's in the bag?"

Mitch turned red and tried to distract her. "Listen, Miriam," he said, "I thought Melissa was going to leave her bedroom curtains, but she took them with her for the dorm. . . . Do you know where I can get some cheap?"

"There's some ugly purple material in the hall closet leftover from when Mother made Manfred's shepherd costume."

"You think Mom would make me some curtains?"

"Did you see the Christmas pageant? Manfred didn't look like a shepherd. He looked like an eggplant! I could make better drapes than *her*."

"I thought you flunked sewing."

"Only because the teacher hated me."

Mitch remembered one of Miriam's sewing projects. "Oh, what a beautiful furniture cover," Mrs. Dietrich had said, spreading the lime-green cloth over the back of the recliner. "And just the right size!" Miriam stormed up the stairs, crying. They didn't learn for weeks that the "furniture cover" was a pair of culottes Miriam had made for herself.

"I suppose you'd charge me for making the curtains?" said Mitch.

"Oh, yes."

"How much? Remember, I'm only making minimum wage at Mac's."

Miriam thought for a long time, inclining her head this way and that as if measuring the window in her mind. Finally she said, "Thirty dollars."

"Forget it!" said Mitch. "I'd rather make them myself."

So he did. He suspected they were the only drapes in the world hemmed with staples. And he wouldn't win any prizes for using a paper punch to make the holes for hanging. But that night, when they were drawn and he sat alone in the privacy of his own room, Mitch felt proud. Now he could pick his nose if he wanted. He could dance across the room naked. The possibilities were endless.

He settled back with a science-fiction book, the *Playboy* magazine on his bedside table. He adjusted the music on the stereo, then took out a Snickers bar.

A few weeks later Miriam knocked on Mitch's door. "Will you be eating dinner with us any night next week?" she demanded.

Mitch opened the door a crack. "*Next week?* Why do you want to know?"

"Because I'll be on KP duty, and I have no intention of setting a place for you night after night if you're not coming downstairs."

Lately Mitch had gotten into the habit of taking his

dinner plate upstairs to eat at his desk. It was quieter, and he wasn't subjected to any of Millard's "what if" dialogues as he ate. "I'll eat up here," he told Miriam. "I wouldn't want you to kill yourself setting that extra place."

"Bah!" she said, leaning heavily against the door. "You can joke if you want, but those people are working me to the bone."

"Yeah, it's a real hassle having to set the table and wash the dishes *one week out of every two months*."

"Look at my hands," said Miriam, thrusting them through the crack in the door. "I've got dishpan hands! I'm not even sixteen and I've got the hands of a ninety-year-old woman."

Mitch could hear some of the younger kids running up the stairway, so he closed the door, saying, "Well, I'm kind of busy, Miriam."

The kids were outside his door now too. All their voices blended into a single voice whose words came at Mitch too loud and too fast: "Was that Mitch?—Mitch, you in there?—Hi Mitch!—Mitch, you on punishment? Is that why you stay there?—No, dummy, Daddy said at dinner he's going through a stage—Mom thinks you smoke in there, Mitch!" He pressed his palms against the door, feeling it vibrate with their words. "I don't smoke," Mitch whispered, then louder: "I may stay in this room *for the rest of my life*!"

From the other side of the door, Mitch heard Miriam reply, "I wouldn't blame you if you did."

Miriam was sitting with Mr. and Mrs. Dietrich when Mitch came down to breakfast one morning in December. The little kids had already left for school. "Hello, stranger," said Mr. Dietrich.

"The return of the prodigal son," said Miriam, then challenged her mother: "Do you know what 'prodigal' means?"

"Mitch, you look like you haven't slept in days," said Mrs. Dietrich, ignoring her daughter's question.

Mitch grunted into his corn flakes. He had stayed up until four A.M., and now his eyes were refusing to focus. It was difficult to get up for school when the purple drapes made the room as dark as midnight at eight thirty A.M.

"I think you spend entirely too much time alone in that room," said Mrs. Dietrich.

It was the same old story. Mitch moaned. "Mom, I love you, but—"

Mrs. Dietrich sighed and wiped up some toast crumbs. "What I'd give to hear that phrase just once without a 'but' on the end of it."

Mitch repeated, "I love you, but you just don't understand."

"Everything's got a butt on the end of it," Miriam remarked. "From a cigarette to the human body."

"Miriam!"

31

"Why does everyone pick on me?" said Miriam, pushing a loaded spoon of Cocoa Puffs into her mouth.

"Mom, I'm just trying to say you can't understand what it's like to finally have a room of my own after seventeen years. It's great."

"You just don't understand teenage boys, Marge," said Mitch's dad.

"Or teenage girls," muttered Miriam, heading for the door.

Even though Mitch finished his corn flakes, brushed his teeth, and gathered together his school-books before leaving the house, he caught up with Miriam less than two blocks away. She always moved slowly, as if she were walking through water. "Don't try to comfort me," she said without even turning to acknowledge him. "Breakfast with *them* has already ruined my day."

"Don't be dramatic."

"You know what I'd like to get them for Christmas?" she said. "A psychiatric evaluation at the Mercy Health Center. How much do you think that would run?"

"More than you could afford. Besides, *they* don't need psychiatric help."

"You're implying that *I* do?"

Mitch didn't answer. If she knew what was going on in *his* head, she'd think *he* was crazy. What would she say if he told her that, as much as he loved the room, there were times when he *hated* it?

That there were some nights when the walls seemed to close in on him, making his heart beat too fast. What would she say if she knew there were times he didn't *like* to be alone?

"Let's cut school," Mitch said suddenly.

"What?" Miriam pushed back her hair and stared at him.

"Really!" said Mitch, getting excited. "I've got some money. We can go downtown and have lunch, then go to a show."

"You and me?" For a second Miriam looked like she was going to cry.

"Let's do it."

"I want to," said Miriam. "I really want to."

"Come on, we've never skipped before. It'll be fun."

Miriam, hunched into her black pea jacket, stood indecisive for thirty seconds. For twenty-nine seconds, Mitch knew there was a possibility; but after they hit the half-minute mark without speaking, they started trudging toward school.

"Oh, well," said Mitch, after a moment. "It was fun thinking about it."

"That's the problem with this family," Miriam muttered. "We just don't know how to have fun."

Mitch could hear a wind moaning outside his window. Usually on nights like this he felt warm and happy within his own cocoon, but tonight was different. The reading lamp seemed to bake his skin;

maybe someone had forgotten to dial down the furnace. He pulled back the quilt, but immediately felt too cold. He twisted the radio dial, listening for something that wasn't there. The clock said three ten A.M., and he wondered if he were the only person awake in the whole city.

He tried reading the interview in the new *Playboy*. He looked at Miss February. He picked up a paperback he'd been trying to finish all week. A cover quote said it was "heartwarming," but as he read, Mitch made gagging noises. The last line of the book was "And he smiled and smiled and smiled." Mitch threw it across the bedroom in disgust. Anybody who "smiled and smiled and smiled" probably needed psychiatric help.

He got up and stretched, but didn't feel as if he could stretch hard enough. There was an itch coming from the inside of his chest, as if at any second a pair of hands was going to split his body open from the inside and a new Mitch would step out into the room, whole.

I've been reading too much science fiction, he thought.

He wasn't sure what was wrong exactly. He just knew a Snickers bar wouldn't cure it this time. From all the psychology books and magazines he'd read, he tried to diagnose his own case, but the only word that came to mind was claustrophobia. "That's silly," he said aloud. "For seventeen years I'm stuffed into a bedroom with a million brothers, and now that I've got my own room, I feel like I'm suffocating?"

He moved to the window and pulled back the purple drapes. It was the first time he had opened them in five months. Large, wet snowflakes splashed onto the windowpane, but he looked past them into the darkness. He looked beyond the back fence, at the house behind the Dietrichs'; it belonged to old Mr. Sims, who had lived there as long as Mitch could remember. There was a light burning in a downstairs window. So, Mitch wasn't the only one up in the city tonight. He looked closer. A girl, about his age, was sitting at the kitchen table, reading a book and eating a bowl of ice cream. She had dark hair and wore a pink robe. Mitch had no idea who she was or what she was doing in Mr. Sims's house. He didn't know what book she was reading or what flavor ice cream she was eating. He only knew that she was someone like him.

Her name was Sara Gilchrist, and her family had moved into Mr. Sims's house in December, a couple months after Mr. Sims died. This was what she told Mitch late the next afternoon when he "accidentally" ran into her on the sidewalk in front of her house.

"Mr. Sims died? You've got to be kidding," said Mitch.

"Why would I be kidding?" Face to face, Mitch

could see that Sara was very pretty, with wide eyes and an easy smile.

"No, I believe you! I just can't believe it. I mean I . . ." The words were getting all twisted on his tongue. It felt like a long time since he'd had a real conversation. Sara was edging toward the car with a small briefcase in her hand. He didn't know what to say to stop her. "So, what school do you go to?" he asked.

"Sleepwalker!" she said, then laughed. "I go to West Grove, same as you." Since he hadn't mentioned he went there, he wondered how she knew. She answered the question before he asked it: "In fact, we're in three classes together!"

Mitch gasped. "I can't believe it!"

"Open your eyes and look around!" she said.

He didn't remember seeing any new girls in his classes these last few months, but then again he spent a lot of class time just trying to keep his eyes open. The late nights were definitely taking a toll. "You must have thought I was stuck-up."

She considered this. Mitch liked that. She didn't just say yes or no; she thought it over seriously. "Maybe a little bit," she said.

"I'm not though, really. I'm the most down-to-earth guy in that whole school, really. I'm really, really a nice guy," he said, thinking: a really, really, really nice guy who doesn't know any other word but "really." Geez.

"Really, really nice, huh?" said Sara. "Well, say hi

36

to me in physics tomorrow and maybe I'll believe you." Her eyes crinkled around the corners when she smiled.

Mitch didn't want to wait for tomorrow. "Do you think we could go out for a hamburger or something?"

"Well . . ." Again, she looked thoughtful. "Not tonight. Definitely not tonight. I've got my art class." She removed a little notebook from her briefcase, and he could see colored pencils inside. The wind rattled the notebook pages as she thumbed through them. "Well, tomorrow I've got ballet class, and Friday night there's a Special Olympics committee meeting. Saturday I'll be working at the hospital all day, and Sunday . . . well, I could squeeze you in Sunday night, I guess."

Squeeze me in? Mitch was too amazed to feel insulted. All day he'd been carrying around a picture of a lonely girl who liked to stay up late and read books, only to learn she had a busier agenda than the U.N. "Sunday sounds good," he said.

That night Mitch sat down to dinner with the rest of the family and even lingered, listening to a lengthy "You'll never guess what happened at school today" story from Marigold. Finally, when everyone else at the table was done talking, Mitch said, "I just found out today that old Mr. Sims died."

Mrs. Dietrich, who was in the midst of wiping up Maude's spilled milk, said, "But Mitch, that happened months ago."

"I know. But I just found out. Where was I when it happened?"

"Probably up in your room," said Miriam.

The first time Sara saw Mitch's bedroom, she was impressed that he'd decorated it himself. "Are these the famous handmade drapes?" she asked, pulling them open and flooding the room with sunlight. "You should keep them open like this. It really makes the room look bigger."

Mitch looked around, blinking. Yes, the room did look bigger. It also looked dustier.

"I think the way a room is decorated really tells a lot about the person who lives there," said Sara. "Now, I look at those posters of clouds and I see . . . someone who's interested in freedom. Am I right?"

Mitch nodded. Actually he just liked pictures of clouds.

"Now the books—wow, you've got a lot of books—well, *they* indicate that you're well read."

"Brilliant deduction," he said, smiling.

"Wait, there's more. The books may also mean that—"

Just then they heard voices on the other side of the door.

"Pests!" yelled Mitch. "You kids get away from the door!"

Footsteps went stumbling down the hallway, and Sara said, "You should have let them come in."

"They're a nuisance."

"Well, you know how kids feel about big brothers," she said.

Mitch didn't know what to say, because he suddenly remembered *exactly* how kids felt about big brothers—and how it felt when Matt and Mark used to brush him off. "I guess they're not pests *all* of the time," Mitch admitted.

"Maybe it's 'cause I'm an only child, but I really like being around kids. That's why I want to be a teacher."

A teacher. "Where will you be going to school?" Mitch asked, afraid to learn how far away she'd be going in a few months.

"Brewster College, up north. What about you?"

"Anyplace that will give me a scholarship," he said.

"Apply to Brewster! They've got a good scholarship program."

"I'll check into it," he said. He liked the idea of spending four years close to Sara.

"Oh, yes, you've got to!" she said, grabbing onto his sleeve.

He turned to the window. The bright sunlight made his eyes water. He couldn't believe his good luck. Not a month ago he was sitting up here in the dark, and now there was a girl practically begging him to come away with her.

Sara stood behind his shoulder. "Hey, you can see my house from here!" she said.

"One time I saw you sitting at the kitchen table, reading," Mitch whispered.

She thought for a moment. "I wasn't in my pajamas or anything, was I?"

"Well . . . your robe."

"I'm so embarrassed," she said. And even though she smiled, Mitch had the feeling that the curtains would be firmly drawn in the Gilchrist kitchen from then on.

That night at dinner Manfred announced, "Mitch had a girl in his bedroom today. They were in there with the door locked, and they were laughing."

Some of the older kids said, "Oooooooohh!" and Mr. Dietrich put down his coffee cup. "We don't believe in locked doors at this house. Mitchell, have you put a lock on your bedroom door?"

"No! I just had it shut."

"With a *girl* in there?" said Mrs. Dietrich.

"We weren't *doing* anything. I was just showing her my room."

"You were laughing!" said Manfred. Mitch looked at Manfred, trying to see him through Sara's eyes. The kid wore a too-big, hand-me-down sweater, and he was bouncing up and down in his seat. He probably didn't even know what the fuss was about; he was just glad to be getting some attention.

"Mitch, we do not want you entertaining girls in your bedroom with the door shut," said Mrs. Dietrich.

Mitch nodded miserably, but Miriam disagreed. "I think that Mitch is entitled to his privacy. As long as they aren't disturbing anyone else or she doesn't get knocked up, then—"

"What's knocked up?" said Manfred, and Milton choked on his milk.

"Miriam, go to your room!" said Mr. Dietrich.

"Bah!" Miriam said, getting up.

"If you want to go around sounding like a sheep, that's your prerogative," said Mrs. Dietrich. "But put that dinner plate down. You're not taking it with you."

After dinner Mitch flopped down on his bed. Again the walls seemed to be pushing in on him, and the fact that Sara had been there—right there in his very own room—made him feel restless. He decided to go for a walk. It felt good to move through the spring twilight, taking big gulps of wet fresh air.

When Mitch returned home it was very late. He hadn't bothered to close the drapes since Sara had opened them, so now a puddle of moonlight gleamed on the hardwood floor. He moved to close them but decided not to.

He pushed open the window and stuck his head out, breathing lilacs. The moon made the flowers glow like candlelight. Then he saw the light in the Gilchrists' kitchen. The curtains were open, and Sara sat inside reading a book and eating pudding. When she got up from the table, Mitch was tempted to pull his head back inside, but he didn't. He watched her as she moved toward the window in her robe and stood looking out, waving good-night.

After that, Mitch spent a lot of time at the Gilchrist house, and Sara spent a lot of time at the Dietrichs'. All the Dietrichs liked her except Miriam. The first time Sara stayed for dinner, Miriam groaned, "Just what I need. Another dish to wash."

Sara bought some green plants for Mitch's windowsill and helped him clean his closet. They painted a mural on the wall. Once they learned how much Sara liked kids, Milton, Marvin, Marigold, Muriel, Maude, Manfred, and Millard were in and out of the room almost as much as Mitch was. They soon discovered the location of his Snickers cache—as well as the issues of *Playboy* in his dresser drawer. They were willing not to mention the magazines if Mitch would keep them supplied with Snickers. To avoid being blackmailed, Mitch dumped the *Playboy*s, then continued buying candy for them anyway. He was actually beginning to *like* the kids.

One day, late in May, Miriam passed the open door of the room. The windows were open, and a warm breeze was blowing the wind chimes that hung from the ceiling. "Come on in," said Mitch. "Me and Manfred are playing darts."

Miriam shook her head in disgust. "This room

makes me want to ralph," she said. "Fresh air, fun-and-games, arts and crafts courtesy of Miss Sara! It's like walking into Romper Room. Bah!"

But Mitch liked it. He liked it when the room was noisy and filled with kids, and he liked it when only Sara was there. He liked it late at night, when he was alone. But considering all the time Mitch spent with Sara—at her house, and the park, and the movies—and all the time he spent at her Special Olympics meetings, or taking the community-center psych course, he really wasn't spending too much time in the room anyway.

In August, Mitch went shopping with Sara. She was looking for some material to make drapes for her dorm room. "Is this bizarre or what?" said Mitch. "Drapes are the whole key to our relation-ship. In February, if I hadn't opened my drapes in the middle of the night and seen you sitting there eating ice cream in your kitchen, we never would have met. And if we hadn't met, I wouldn't be going to Brewster. If we hadn't met, I'd probably still be hibernating in that dark room all by my—"

"I doubt that," she said, then held up an orange-and-yellow print. "Why don't you get some too, for your dorm?"

He shook his head. "My drape-making days are over. Besides, I don't intend to spend too much time in my dorm. I'll be in class all day, and out at football

43

games, and visiting my girlfriend. Actually, I plan to spend a *lot* of time visiting my girlfriend."

"Hey, there's Miriam," said Sara, pointing to a heavy figure walking toward the checkout counter. "Hi, Miriam!"

"Bah!" said Miriam.

She dumped a huge armful of material onto the counter. "What a lot of black velvet!" the clerk exclaimed.

"I'm going into the shroud business," said Miriam.

"Are you making a dress?" asked Sara.

"Give me a break—even *I* don't need this much material for a dress!" Arms outstretched, she held the material in the air, disappearing from view.

"Drapes," said Mitch.

Miriam nodded. "Ceiling to floor. Thick. Jet-black. No one's going to see in, and I'm not interested in what's out."

"Drapes?" said Sara. "Oh, for Mitch's room!"

"*My* room," said Miriam. "In two weeks it won't be Mitch's anymore."

Mitch Dietrich was up early that Sunday, packing. In a few hours he would be in a car heading up north to Brewster College. He taped up his last box of paperbacks as the sun began to rise over the top of Sara's house. Slowly the room began to fill with light, and he took one last look around. The walls were bare, the mural had been painted over, the desk was clean and neat.

Already it looked as if Mitch had never lived there.

Until yesterday the room had been filled with sunshine, green plants, Sara, little kids, and a dartboard, but now only the sunshine was left—and Mitch knew Miriam would soon take care of *that*.

He shifted his suitcases and turned the doorknob, to find Miriam sitting on a trunk in the hallway, her arms full of black velvet. "I've been here since six A.M.," she said darkly.

"Why didn't you come in to talk? I was up."

"Because I believe a person should have complete privacy when they are alone in their own bedroom. That room should be their sanctuary, their haven, their refuge, their asylum. And if anyone so much as *looks* into this room besides me in the next twelve months, I'll chop off their heads!"

"Very nice," he said.

"Why don't you leave, so I can take over?" she said.

Mitch bowed at the hip and lifted his arm toward the room, as if he were formally introducing it. "It's all yours."

Then something bizarre happened.

Without a word Miriam threw her arms around him. The force of the hug knocked him against the doorjamb. "Hey, does this mean you're going to miss me?" said Mitch.

"Yeah," Miriam whispered.

"I'll miss you, too," said Mitch.

Miriam pulled away from him, gathering up black

velvet with her face averted. "Bah!" she said, slamming the door from the inside.

With a box under each elbow and a suitcase in each hand, Mitch started down the hall. He wondered how many days or weeks or months would go by before the door opened again. Because he knew it would open again. He didn't look back; he just kept going. And he smiled and smiled and smiled.

Heartbeats

It's spring and the robins are back like Mommy said. We are watering the lawn so it will grow tall and green. Then a lady comes up the driveway. She is tall and green. She is carrying a baby and smoking a cigarette. Hi, the Green Lady says, my name's Marie Minotti—we just moved in across the street.

Mommy smiles and says, Oh how nice—I'm Ann Blaine—and who is this little precious?

Oh this is Angie, says the Green Lady, and I've got another one somewheres.

Then this little girl comes zooming up the driveway on a tricycle that goes faster than the Batmobile. The Green Lady reaches out a green arm and grabs the front of the trike. The little girl falls off and that makes me laugh.

This, says the Green Lady, is Lisa.

Lisa has long dark hair and chocolate on her hands and lips. When she hears me laughing, she gets the mad look on her face and says, You're ugly, so I spray her with the hose and she starts to cry.

Paul! Mommy says and grabs both my hands and Lisa goes running and hides her face in a green pants leg.

The Green Lady says, They're both the same age. I'm sure they'll be friends.

* * *

We are on the swings at the park. Lisa says, "And then Janie's mother stopped the Good Humor man and got us a Bon-Joy Cup."

"Oh." I pump harder and harder, trying to get the swing even with the top bar. Out of all the kids in Mrs. Leonard's second-grade class, I like Lisa best. But Lisa is always hanging around with Janie. "Why are you always going over to Janie's house? I live closer."

Lisa's voice is far away because she's swinging way back and I'm swinging forwards. She says: "Because Janie's my best friend."

"Why can't I be your best friend?"

"Because girls are best friends with girls"—pump—"and boys are best friends with boys."—pump—"Oh, no!"

"What's wrong? Didja get pinched by the swing?"

"No. Here comes Janie again. Let's go!" We fly off the swings while they are still in the air. My feet sting when they hit the ground, but I move quick so the swing won't come back and hit me in the head. We run to the bushes, and Lisa says, "Is she gone?"

I climb to the top of the jungle gym. "I don't see her."

"Good."

So we get on the seesaw: up and down, up and down. I go up. "I thought Janie was your best friend."

"She is." I plunge down.

"How come you don't want her to see you?"

Lisa's face flies down in front of mine. "She's my best friend, but I like playing with you better."

I dig my heels into the dirt to stop the seesaw. Now we are face to face; both of us even. "You do, Lisa? Really?"

*   *   *

"Do you want to stay for lunch, Paul?" Mrs. Minotti puts down her cigarette and heads for the refrigerator.

"No thanks, Mrs. M. I just came to get Lisa so she could see the garden. The corn's starting to come up."

"She'll be down as soon as she changes out of her church clothes," she says, peering into a plastic bowl as if she's not sure it's the leftover tuna salad.

"Don't fix nothing for me, honey," Grandma Minotti says. "That roast pork you fix last night gave me a feeling right here." She points to the center of her chest. She is seventy-one, Italian, and blind in one eye.

49

"Cripes! There's no pleasing you, is there—" Mrs. Minotti begins, but she is interrupted by Lisa and Angie flying down the stairs. They haven't finished changing yet. Angie is in her underwear and Lisa's wearing a play smock with her church skirt. "She punched me! That little brat punched me!" Lisa shrieks. Angie hides behind her mother's legs.

"What happened?" Mrs. Minotti sighs.

"She walked all over my crayons, so I slapped her, then she punched me . . . right here!" Lisa jerks her thumb up to her chest.

Grandma Minotti makes little *tsk* sounds. "For a woman to get hurt in the breast is very bad."

"My God, Mother Minotti! She's only nine. She doesn't have breasts!" To prove her point, Mrs. Minotti grabs ahold of Lisa and jerks her smock up toward her shoulders. "See?"

Lisa lets out a howl. "Ma! Maaaa!" she shrieks. "Why did you—? He looked. *He looked!*"

"No, I didn't," I say, but she is running up the stairs, crying.

Grandma Minotti is muttering: "Oh, for a woman to get hurt in the breast is very—"

"Would you *shut up*!" says Mrs. Minotti, throwing a Tupperware container onto the kitchen table. "I've had just about enough today—"

I walk out the door into a very bright day. Lisa is wrong. I didn't "look." As soon as her mother grabbed ahold of her smock, I knew what was coming. I knew, and I shut my eyes. Even though her shirts were always so big you could see right down them every time she bent over. Even though a few years ago she used to swim topless in the backyard pool. Even with all that, I shut my eyes when Mrs. Minotti grabbed Lisa's smock.

I don't know why.

* * *

"Are you okay?"

I roll over and look at Lisa. Her head is blocking the sun. "I'm okay."

"Are you sure?"

"I said I'm okay!"

"You don't have to yell."

"Leave me alone then."

"What were those guys saying?" she asks.

"Stuff. Who cares?"

"Stuff about me?"

"You and me. What difference does it make?"

"Did you tell them to go to hell?" she asks.

"No, I just told them to cut it out."

"But they kept saying stuff, so you hit them?"

"No, they kept saying stuff, then *they* hit *me.*"

"Does it hurt?" I don't answer, so she says, "Okay, okay. It was a dumb question."

"That's right." I shut my eyes, trying to ignore the flashes of color exploding under my eyelids.

I hear her voice: "Don't worry. Next year, in junior high, it won't be like that."

"Lisa, go home without me."

"But we always—"

"Go ahead. We can walk home together some other time."

* * *

I stand at the Minottis' back door on a cloud-covered Saturday afternoon. Lisa holds the door open for me. "Long time no see," she says coldly.

"Come on, Lisa, I see you every day in school."

"Long time no come over, then."

Bending down to take off my shoes, I can see Mrs. Minotti's cigaretted profile watching TV in the other room. "Well, you know how it is, with school and everything—" I begin to explain.

"Yeah, I know," she says sarcastically. "Junior high's so hard that you don't need me until the old algebra starts to trip you up. Did you bring the book?"

"Wait. Don't be this way. I'm not trying to use you or anything. I'll help you with English, history, Spanish, anything."

"Are you saying I need help in all those subjects?"

"Lisa, don't be like this."

"Like what?" She waits. "Don't I have the *right*? We're friends for years, then—just because a few grade-school punks beat you up—it's good-bye Lisa." I wince. "Well, don't think I've been sitting around waiting for you. I've made a whole load of new friends. Right now, they're dancing in the basement and I want you to meet them."

A quiver of jealousy runs up my throat as I follow her down the stairs. Against the wall, I see silhouettes of dancing figures. I can hear them clapping and stomping, laughing and screaming, even over the blare of Michael Jackson's music. And then I see the dancers: eight little kids moonwalking across the basement. And none of them older than ten-year-old Angie.

One pudgy little kid jumps forward. "How old are yooooooouuuu!" he shrieks.

"A hundred and nine," I say. I'm in no mood to deal with little kids.

"He's fourteen," snaps Lisa. "And watch out. You might grow up to be just like him."

* * *

Lisa is running a business. "I'm not a baby-sitter," she insists. "I'm an entrepreneur!"

Officially, it's a baby-sitting service, but Lisa always refers to her business as a "child-care center." It's kind of neat. I mean, I'm always coming up with these great ideas on how to make a lot of money, but that's all they are: ideas. They never get off the ground. Lisa got an idea and did something about it.

We're playing tag with the kids—dashing around behind the heater and furnace in the basement—and it suddenly strikes me. "Gosh, Lisa, this is just like when *we* were kids."

She stops running. "No," she says. "It's different."

* * *

"Brian, let go of Martha's hair," says Lisa.

Brian gives the hair another tug, then another.

Each time he yanks it, Martha gives a high-pitched squeal like a piglet.

"Here, Martha, why don't you cover your hair with this," says Lisa, taking a hat decorated with flowers and grapes from the dress-up trunk. She bends down to tie the yellow ribbon under the little girl's chin. It's the first time I've realized Lisa is pretty: Her skin is clear, her hair looks soft.

Martha squeals as Brian tries to pull the hat off her head. "Oh, did you want to wear an Easter bonnet too, Brian?" says Lisa. "Leave Martha alone and come put this one on." She holds out a pink-and-white hat covered with tall purple feathers.

Brian folds his arms over his chest. "No way," he says, then marches off. Even though I've just been sitting there—not involved at all—I feel like the victory is mine, too. For a second, I have this tremendous urge to touch Lisa's face.

"I wanna eat!" Patty yells.

There's a chorus of "me too's" all around the basement, and Lisa looks at her watch. "No, no," she says. "It's only ten minutes past seven o'clock. We won't have Hi-C and cookies until seven thirty. Does anyone know how many minutes that is?"

"Twenty," a voice says. I am sitting there thinking: Forget the kids, look at me! Pay attention to me! I feel like a five-year-old with a new baby brother, begging for attention. "Twenty minutes," the same voice repeats.

"Paul! Cut it out," Lisa says to me. "I'm asking the kids."

* * *

We're playing Monster in the Dark.

The lights are out and everyone's running, looking for a place to hide. I stumble through the darkness and crawl behind the basement sink. My hand touches a tiny hand, and Martha shrieks. "Sorry about that, kid," I say, and run across the room. Brian is on the top of the stairs counting out loud, "Ninety-four, ninety-five, ninety-six." I dive into the space between the couch and the basement wall. I can feel the cold concrete beneath my sweatshirt, and there is a cobweb touching my face. Two feet run past me as Brian yells, "Ready or not, here I come!"

I hear the *whoomp* before I feel it. Someone has jumped right on top of me. Stupid kids! Then I realize it's not one of the kids. It's Lisa. "Sorry," she whispers, climbing off me.

I reach back and grab her arm. "It's okay," I whisper. "Stay. Brian's coming."

Through the back of my sweatshirt, I can feel her on top of me, facedown on my back. She's soft. She smells like lemon pudding, and I feel hot and cold at the same time. My heart begins to bang against my rib cage. Can she feel it? Suddenly, I realize I can feel her heart beating too, its rhythm off just a little bit from mine. . . . And then I can only hear one heartbeat. Is it just mine, or are they both beating at the same time now? Lisa reaches down and touches my cheek and all of a sudden Brian is standing over us. "C'mon you guys, run! Run! . . . Hey, don't you know how to play this game?" he says in his little-kid voice.

We get up and start to run, but before we do, Lisa touches my hand and I touch hers.

*   *   *

Grandma Minotti is clucking her tongue and shaking her head. "Fourteen is *too* young. Fourteen much too young," she keeps saying over and over.

"My God!" says Mrs. Minotti, throwing the *TV Guide* down. "They're just going to a dance, they're not getting married!" She is dressed all in blue. It's her trademark to dress all in one color. I remember the first time I saw her—she was dressed all in green. It seems like a hundred years ago.

Lisa's kid sister, Angie, is bopping around the room trying to get someone's attention. She tugs on her mother's arm. "Can I go on dates when I'm fourteen, Ma? Huh?"

"We'll worry about that when you're fourteen."

"Grandma Minotti says—"

"Grandma Minotti doesn't know what the hell she's talking about. Now let go of my arm, Angie."

I sit on the edge of the couch—the couch I've jumped on, walked over, spilled grape pop on—as if I've never been in the house before. Then Lisa

56

enters the room in a yellow dress. "You look great!" I say, jumping up.

Mr. Minotti emerges from behind his newspaper to say, "Be back by eleven." To be perfectly truthful, I've forgotten he was even in the room. It happens a lot. He seems to get swallowed up by all the Minotti women.

As we walk to the dance, I am only conscious of Lisa beside me, conscious of her hand in mine. I know I'm going to kiss her tonight. "We could have gotten a ride from my dad," Lisa says.

"But it's such an incredible night. . . ."

"We would have gotten there quicker," she says, then stops and turns to me. "I have a proposition."

My heart skips a beat.

"I want you to be my partner in the business— you're over all the time anyway. But we've got to get something settled first. I pay my ma fifteen dollars a week for the use of the basement. That comes right off the top. Then comes the money for snacks. Whatever's left over we split, fifty-fifty. How does that sound?" Her speech sounded rehearsed; she said it fast.

"Terrific. It's a deal." I don't know what else to say. I almost stick my hand out to shake on the deal. We are standing under a streetlight and she has a peculiar half smile on her lips, as if expecting me to say something else.

This is a dream, I think, as my head slowly tilts

downward and hers lifts to meet mine. *I'm just dreaming*, I think, as my eyes start to close and I feel her shoulders beneath my hands.

But when our lips finally touch, I know it's not a dream. No. I feel as if I've been dreaming all my life, and it wasn't until this moment that I came awake.

* * *

We are holding hands, and when Lisa gestures, both our hands gesture. Now they go up in midair and shake three times as Lisa says, "We've been going together for eight months and it's still as good as it was at the beginning." We are at a party, talking to a group of kids. She continues: "Would you believe we've never had a fight in those eight months?"

I look around the room and see all kinds of people divided into couples. It feels good to be part of a pair.

"He wanted to branch out, start some other child-care centers around the city," Lisa is saying. "But I said, who's going to train teenagers to run the other centers? How are we going to pay them? Then, the IRS would probably step in and—" Lisa is talking about her favorite topic: the business. "I said, Paul, just forget it! Not that I have to worry, because if it's up to Paul it won't get done. He's the dreamer. *I'm* the doer! He's got all kinds of plans, but no ambition."

I draw my hand away from hers.

"What's wrong?" she says.

"Nothing."

"Paul, tell me what's wrong."

The rest of the kids are talking about a concert now, so I reply, "What you were just saying."

"About the business?"

"About me. You made me sound like a real loser."

"You're not a loser," she says, reaching for my hand.

"He's a big dreamer, he's got no ambition," I quote.

"Well, it's true. You *are* a dreamer! You *don't* have any ambition!"

"I've got all kinds of ambition! When I think what I can do with my life, I'm just filled with—I don't know—it's like I could do everything. *You* make it sound like I'm a big zero."

My "you" doesn't sit well with Lisa. I can see it in her eyes. "Filled with ambition?" she laughs. "That's not all you're full of! Believe me, Paul, what you *think* you can do and what you *can* do are two different things."

"Meaning what?" I say.

"My God, you're so sensitive!"

"I don't have to listen to this."

"You *don't* have to," she says, getting up. "I'm leaving."

She storms out of the party.

"I thought she said you never fight," some girl says.

59

Between bites of roast beef Mom says, "I haven't seen Lisa lately. How is she?"

"How should I know?" I snarl.

"Sensitive subject?" she probes.

"What's that supposed to mean—sensitive? 'Sensitive' just means you feel things. What's wrong with feeling things?"

"Nothing's wrong with it," says Dad. "We just don't like to see you feeling bad."

"We got into a fight, okay? It was nothing." Nothing? Yeah, nothing compared to how I'm feeling now. I don't know whether it's all over for good or what, and I hate not knowing. I get up from the table.

"Where are you going?"

"I've got to straighten something out," I say.

As the door slams behind me, I hear Dad sigh, "Young love."

Love? That's not even funny. Love is valentines and romance and laughing and kissing. Love doesn't have anything to do with what I'm feeling now: sick, cranky, falling behind in school.

It's cold and dark and I stamp my feet as I knock on the Minottis' back door. Someone turns on the porch light and I see my reflection in the window. Then Lisa pulls back the curtain, and I still think I'm seeing my reflection in the window: Her expression matches everything I've been feeling for the past week and a half. She opens the door and comes outside. For a second, neither of us says anything, then we both say "I'm sorry" at the same time, then laugh because we said it at the same time. We come together like we've never been apart. Without coats, we stand outside in the black October night, and I feel that a part of myself that's been missing for a long time has been returned.

Yeah, it's love.

* * *

"So what are you thankful for this year?" I ask.

"I'm thankful you only ask clichéd questions like that once a year," Lisa says.

"No, seriously."

"I *am* serious. I'm also thankful there's no school till Monday." We are walking home from school on the day before Thanksgiving. The sky looks like it was done with gray watercolors.

"I'm thankful I passed my driver's-ed test," I say.

"Me too. Pretty soon we won't have to be chauffeured everywhere by the parents."

I don't say it out loud, but I'm also thankful everything's so good between us. It's been over a year since that dumb fight . . . and every day has been better than the last. Sometimes when I'm with Lisa, my heart feels like it's expanding beyond my ribcage and filling my whole body.

All of a sudden she's running past me, her arms outstretched in the wind like a November butterfly. That is the difference between the two of us. I always get these storybook, movieland ideas of running through falling leaves, but I always restrain myself.

Lisa has probably never thought about dancing through leaves before—but when she gets the idea, she does it.

Lisa can make me feel anything—*do* anything—and suddenly I'm beside her; we're running through the park, screaming and shouting like two crazy people. But we don't care. I feel like I could take off in the wind like a kite. Lisa dives into a huge pile of leaves, and even though I want to keep going, I plunge in too. We lie there with our eyes shut, trying to breathe. My heart is pounding, and I swear I can feel the spin of the earth beneath my chest. My eyes still closed, I reach out my hand and . . . meet Lisa's in midair.

I feel like my heart could burst.

* * *

It's a perfect night. It's the first time I've been in a Catholic church, but I'm not really paying attention to the surroundings. I watch her singing, hear her voice above all the others, and know she is mine. Then, as we walk together over the snow-packed sidewalk, silent under the sparkling black sky, I know I've never been closer to another person in my life.

Her family is at an aunt's party, so the house is ours. Inside, we sit on the carpet in front of the window. She gets big goblets from the cupboard and fills them too high with dark-red wine. We clink them together, like people in the movies. "Merry Christmas," she says.

"Merry Christmas."

I am suddenly struck by the fact that Lisa is not pretty anymore. She is beautiful. With her back to the window, she looks like a picture in a frame. The blue-black sky, the stars, her dark hair folded around her shoulders, her eyes. Her lips are as red as her skirt, and though her blouse is white, her skin is even whiter as she begins to undo the buttons, one by one. And I know that if she continues, we will not stop this time. I can feel my heart beating in my throat and palms. I want her with every jarring beat of my heart. I want her . . . but do I want everything to change? I want things to be as they are at this very moment. Can't they stay this way a while longer?

She senses my hesitation and her blouse falls open as she leans over and takes my face between her hands. "What's wrong?" she asks.

They are the hardest words I've ever spoken. "Lisa, I'm not sure we're ready for this. . . ."

"Oh *I* am," she whispers, and she seems to grow larger and larger in front of me, blocking out the window and the night and the stars, "*I* am."

* * *

Wheezing and gasping, we complete the first half of our jog. We circle the swings and seesaw in the park and head back around. "I've got to get in shape for graduation," Lisa pants.

"You *are* in shape. But you'd be in better shape if you gave up the cancer sticks."

"Shove it," she says, and I'm spared further comments because she is winded.

Later, in the car, she's in a hurry to get a McDonald's breakfast.

"So we can replace all the calories we just ran off?" I say. "Hold on a second so I can change out of this T-shirt." I start to pull it off and stop. "Well, you don't have to stare at me," I say.

"Why can't I look at you?"

"I don't know. . . ."

"Paul, I see you without your shirt *all the time.*"

All the time? Well, five times since Christmas. I peel off the T-shirt, deciding I'm just being stupid. . . . It's just that my chest always looks so white and thin and dumb-looking. At least it does to me.

Lisa laughs, and for a second I think she *is* laughing at my chest, but she says, "We really are a lot alike. Remember the time *I* threw a fit because my mom pulled my shirt off in front of you?"

"Yeah," I say. But there's one difference. Back then, I shut my eyes. This time, she just keeps looking.

* * *

"I'm sorry," says Lisa, leaning against the outside wall of the funeral parlor. Her head is down and she's taking big gulps of wet March air. "I don't know what happened. I thought I was going to faint in there or something."

"It's okay, it's okay," I say, patting her and making soothing noises. I am touched—almost to the point of tears myself. "These things are always hard to get through," I say.

64

"I just kept thinking how lonely it must be to die. Then it hit me: someday it's going to happen to me. And it can happen so quick: a car accident, a gunshot, a heart attack. And that's it. Like with Grandma Minotti. One minute she was sitting there complaining, and the next thing I know, she's dead. It happens that fast. I mean, can you imagine how alone you must feel when you're dying? There's nobody—I mean nobody at all—who can do it with you. I don't want to live my life alone, so why should I have to die that way?"

"Oh, Lisa, I know," I say, tears now running down my own cheeks. "Don't think about it, please. Don't worry. I know you're scared."

"I am scared. Really scared," she says, burying her face in my shoulder. "Hold me tighter."

We hold each other in the gray twilight, and I feel an almost unbearable closeness. Suddenly she stiffens and pulls away, trying to laugh. "All right, enough of this, huh? I must have looked like an idiot running out of there like that." She pulls a cigarette from her purse and flicks her lighter. She knows I hate it when she smokes. She only started a couple months ago—and I often wonder if she does it just to irritate me.

"Lisa," I say, watching her trying to be brave, flicking the lighter again and again because her hands are shaking. "Lisa, it's okay to be scared. You don't have to be strong."

She whirls around. "Yeah, I do!" she says. "I do

have to be strong. That's how I am. That's how I want to be. Especially when I'm with you!"

"I'm not weak!"

"The hell you aren't! You're about the weakest guy I've ever met. Name one other guy who'd start crying just because I'm crying." I open my mouth, but she continues: "Don't get me wrong, Paul. I *do* love you, but one of us has to be the strong one— and that's *me*! So just accept me as I am!"

We stare at each other. It's a standoff. "Now let's go back in," she says, and we walk back into the funeral home.

* * *

Things are different for graduating seniors. We look and act different from anyone else. Lisa's hair is short now—"I wanted a change," she said—and the new Lisa is striking: thinner, neater, almost streamlined in the clothes she bought over Easter vacation. Me? Sometimes I think I'll never change.

As seniors we can talk to freshmen in the cafeteria without losing status. Lisa is talking to a couple of kids who think they're hot stuff for going together a month and a half, and she's trying to conduct some kind of romance seminar. "It's rocky," she tells the blond couple. "But you know, with Paul and me, we're best friends first, lovers second, and business partners third. We've had problems of course—Paul is so sensitive, you wouldn't believe! But I guess opposites must attract, because here we are."

"How long have you been going together?" asks the girl.

"Oh, forever and ever," Lisa says.

Sometimes it seems like it. We've known each other since we were four, after all. I look back and all my memories are quick images, like photographs. My life isn't divided into years, or months, or even days. Each of my memories just encompasses a moment—a heartbeat or two. Lisa and the Green Lady, me and Lisa on the seesaw, Lisa by the window on Christmas Eve. The funny thing is, I don't have any memories all my own. I wonder what I'd be if we'd never met. I know I could do so much with my life if I had the chance—just like I know that Lisa is a part of me.

My thoughts are interrupted by the freshman boy. "Are you guys going to get married?"

"Probably," Lisa answers quickly.

*   *   *

When I see the envelope from State in the mailbox, I tear it up. It's better not to know how they answered. It's better the way things are going to work out: both of us at the community college, both of us working at the post office in the evening. Like Lisa says, "What's the point of going away to school when you don't even know how you'll like it? Go here for a couple years and see. Who knows, you might not even want to continue."

She has a point. Besides, I could never think of

leaving her. I need her. She is the other half of me.

I throw away the pieces of the State letter and I'm glad. If I keep them, I might be tempted to tape them together someday.

* * *

Red light. Lisa slams on the brakes and the car comes to an abrupt halt on Cowan Street. "God, it's hot!" she says, rolling down the window.

"Yeah." Graduation is only four days away. It's a happy-sad time, an introspective period that really doesn't—shouldn't—leave room for thinking about the heat or the sun bouncing off car hoods.

And then I see them: a boy and a girl in an old convertible. They are stopped at the light too, but coming from the other direction. And there is something about them that makes me keep looking. I guess it's because they look so happy. He's driving, and she's sitting next to him with her bare feet stretched up on the dashboard. They are both smiling and laughing, and she seems to be singing along with the radio or something. Their hair is windblown and they look like they belong together.

"Lisa?"

"What?" She turns to me irritably, as if I've interrupted some great inner thought process, when I know all she's been thinking about is the heat.

"Look at that couple up there. In the convertible."

"Yeah? What about them?"

"I don't know . . . they look so . . ."

"So *what*?"

"I don't know. . . . Happy, I guess."

"Oh cripes! Don't start that perfect-love stuff again—please. In the first place, they are not a couple. You should know just by looking at them that they're brother and sister—Rick and Joan Buckman. They're juniors over at Saint Matthew's. They're twins, not *lovers*."

"Oh, Lisa," I say, turning to the window.

"And secondly—" But I don't listen to secondly. I am too interested in looking at our reflections in the side window: Lisa and me, me and Lisa. Now there's a resemblance. We really do look a lot alike: the same short, dark hair, the same light shirt and jeans, the same angry eyes. Maybe Lisa is right. Maybe this is what love is, what the two of us have. Maybe there is no perfect love. Maybe it's time to stop dreaming and face reality. But my heart starts beating wildly like a too-big bird flapping its wings in a small wooden cage. Calm down, I think. Isn't it enough that we have each other?

Green light. Me and Lisa move on.

Three O'clock Midnight

Six nineteen P.M., and Sid Linwood, former Siamese twin of Debbie Kendricks, surveys the rubble that was once his life. He is depressed. It has been exactly ninety-one days since he and Debbie were forcibly separated by greedy parents (hers), whose cold-hearted pursuit of the great American dollar bill led them to—of all places—the ironically named Romance, Nevada.

It has not been a happy time for Sid.

For ninety-one days he has sighed and stared out windows. He has seen every movie in Detroit at least twice. He has gotten so far ahead in his class assignments that he could skip school from now (December 31) to his birthday (April 10) and it wouldn't matter. This will be the first New Year's Eve in two years he has spent alone.

"Hey, Mom," he yells down the hallway. "Have you seen my 'Life's a Bitch' sweatshirt?"

"Oh, no you don't!" His mother's head, when it pops from her bedroom door, looks enormous. She spent all afternoon at the beauty parlor, and now her hair looks like it's pumped with air. "You are not wearing that awful sweatshirt ever again."

There is something ominous about those words "ever again."

"Mom? . . . Mom?" But she ducks back through her bedroom door. He can hear perfume being sprayed. "Mommy!" He has not called her that since he was six (ten years ago), so it's a surefire attention getter. Within seconds she's hurrying down the hall, calling, "Sid? Sid, dear? Is something wrong?"

He confronts her with folded arms and narrowed eyes. "What did you mean, I won't wear that shirt *ever again*?"

"Sid, that shirt is disgusting and I don't think—"

"*Debbie* gave that sweatshirt to me."

"I don't care if Princess Margaret Rose gave it to you. I don't like it."

"It doesn't make any difference whether *you*—" He pauses. "Who is Princess Margaret Rose?"

"Queen Elizabeth's sister."

"Why would Queen Elizabeth's sister give me a sweatshirt?"

"She wouldn't, but that's beside the point." She

71

puts her fingertips to the outer edges of her jet-puffed hair and sighs. "Oh, Sid, whenever we try to talk, my head starts spinning. I just don't like that sweatshirt. I don't like the sentiment at all."

"Where *is* it, Mom?"

"Well, I just decided to get rid of it, once and for all. I started to put it in the Goodwill bag, but then I thought, no! No, I will not give that sweatshirt to another boy to wear. A disadvantaged boy at that! Sid, I put your sweatshirt in the incinerator."

He slams the bedroom door shut and throws himself onto the bed. How could she do it? It was *his*! It came from *Debbie*! Life *is* a bitch!

"Now, Sid." Her voice is anxious in the hallway. "Don't make me feel guilty—not on New Year's Eve! I have every intention of taking you shopping tomorrow and—"

His voice is muffled by the pillow. "The stores are closed tomorrow."

"Well, the next day then. I have every intention of replacing that sweatshirt. When I was at Sears this morning I saw some shirts with rock groups on them. You like rock groups."

He raises himself off the pillow. "Which rock groups?"

"Oh . . . all kinds!"

Clearly his mother knows nothing about rock groups. But she'd rather die than admit she doesn't know something. The first flame of anger from the incinerated sweatshirt is cooling off. "They don't, by any chance, have any Partridge Family shirts at Sears, do they, Mom?"

"Why, yes! Yes, I'm almost sure they do! . . . Sid? Sid, dear, why are you making that funny noise?"

Later, she calls to him from the living room. "Sid, come down here. Dickie and I are leaving now."

Dickie is his mother's "beau," a large, balding guy who snorts when he laughs. A few months ago Dickie found out Sid is on the golf team at school, so now he mentions golf every time he sees Sid. Tonight, true to form, he says, "Happy New Year, sport. Bet you can't wait till the snows melts and you're back on the ol' golf course."

Sid gives a noncommittal grunt.

His mother says, "Sid, come give me a New Year's hug. . . . On second thought, don't. This new dress gets wrinkled at the slightest touch." She holds the dress away from her body, and looks over at Dickie.

Dickie picks up a chocolate-covered cherry from the coffee table and unwraps it.

After staring at Dickie for a full forty seconds, Sid's mother says, "Give me a hug anyway, sweetheart. I don't give a flying fig about wrinkles."

Sid gives his mother a hug (even though he *is* still mad at her). When he notices she's staring mournfully at Dickie over his shoulder, he hugs her extra hard.

While Dickie investigates the roof of his mouth with a toothpick, Sid's mother hurries about getting her coat and scarf. She's so excited by her night out, she cannot complete a single sentence:

"We're just going to be at the Methodist Hall, so if you need us . . .

"Sid, what about dinner . . . have you . . . can you find . . . ?

"There's a new *Life* magazine on my bedside table, if you . . .

"But then, you probably have other plans . . . do you . . . ?"

By now Dickie is helping Sid's mother into her coat. "Hey, Gloria," he says, as they exit, "that dress you're wearing sure is wrinkly."

Sid closes the door with a sigh of relief. It is seven twenty-one P.M.

"Now is the winter of my discontent," he says aloud. He doesn't know where he heard that phrase before (he knows it's not original), but it seems a fitting remark for the occasion. He surveys the living room. Lights twinkle on the Christmas tree; red and green candles flicker on the mantel. There is a pile of chocolate-covered-cherry foils on the coffee table.

Tomorrow they will take down the tree, pack up the decorations. Sid's mother has been known to get teary at those times. Suddenly he has an idea: Why not spare her all the extra work—as well as the tears? Besides, it will give him something to do.

Now that he's regained a purpose in life, Sid begins to clear the packages from beneath the tree.

Although most of their Christmas gifts have been put to use by now, there are still a few items left among the pine needles: a bottle of bath salts from Dickie to Mom, a box of golf balls from Dickie to Sid, a Gillette safety razor from Mom to Sid (which Sid may be able to use in about three years if his blond beard continues to come in at its present rate), and a very large, very dark fruitcake from a great-aunt in the Upper Peninsula.

Sid puts the golf balls and safety razor in his bedroom. He takes the bath salts to his mother's room. When he tries to put the fruitcake in the freezer, he has to remove last year's cake to make room for it. "Why does she always send us a fruitcake when she *knows* we hate it?" Sid asked Debbie Kendricks last year. He and Debbie were sitting next to the Christmas tree, side by side, the way they always sat.

Debbie said, "Have you told your aunt you don't like fruitcake?"

"Of course not!"

"If you don't tell her, how do you expect her to know?"

"*Nobody* likes fruitcake!"

"I do," said Debbie, and cut herself a slice.

Sid looks down at last year's fruitcake. It's heavy and frozen and has one thin slice cut from it. Debbie's slice. He would like to save this cake as a souvenir of the Debbie Kendricks Experience, but there really is no place to put it. He decides to cut it up for the birds who hang around the Linwood backyard all winter. His mother is a big bird lover; she's always throwing leftover food onto the lawn for them—anything from breadcrumbs to jars of strawberry jelly, it doesn't matter what. Her attitude is "It's food, they'll eat."

Debbie was over one morning when Sid's mother threw a leftover turkey carcass out the kitchen window. "Oh, Mrs. Linwood, you won't get them to eat that. No way." Sid's mother just smiled and tossed some leftover sweet potatoes over the windowsill. She liked Debbie; she just didn't like her *a lot.*

Debbie's smiling face floats in front of Sid's eyes as he hacks away at the fruitcake, and he doesn't notice the knife sliding across a large frozen cherry and into his thumb until he sees red on his hands. It's an easy excuse for crying. What if he's lost Debbie Kendricks for good?

In the past ninety-one days Sid has written Debbie eighty-nine letters. Debbie has sent him four. Five, if you count the Christmas card last week.

A few weeks ago, tired of blaming the U.S. Postal Service, Sid solemnly swore he was going to go cold turkey: no more Debbie Kendricks. He got up that morning vowing that every time a picture of Debbie appeared behind his eyelids (about every seven seconds) he would push it away. He pushed it away while he showered, he pushed it away at breakfast, he pushed it away on the bus, but when he got to his first class, he spent the whole period writing D.K. + S.L. in his notebook. That night, as usual, he carried Debbie's framed photograph into bed with him. It was a losing battle. He was hooked for life.

Sid shoves the bird-size morsels of fruitcake into a plastic bag and hunts for his boots. They are not in the closet or on the basement landing. He realizes they are probably sitting on top of the clothes drier, where his mother put them last time he came home. (Can it really be that he hasn't been outside in three or four days?) Sid notices Mom's shiny red boots, still wet, sitting on a newspaper in the kitchen. Even his mother gets out of the house more often than he does.

He remembered when his mother's boots used to look huge. Now he can barely squeeze his toes through the top of hers. Still, he won't need them for long—just the two minutes it will take to distribute the birdcake. But what if someone sees him wearing a pair of women's red boots with a half-inch heel? "So what?" he can hear Debbie Kendricks say in his mind's ear.

Debbie had a quick-and-easy answer for every-thing. "Things are seldom what they seem" was one of her favorite expressions. He knew what she meant: The world's too big for us to know all the answers, so don't worry about it. That attitude was one of the best things about Debbie (besides the burnt-orange hair and gold-brown eyes, besides the crackling laugh and steel-trap mind). She was never scared, never bored. When things were going badly, she had an unshakable belief that they'd right them-

77

selves soon enough. Until her parents announced that they were moving to Romance, Nevada. Then she cried and wrote "Dear Abby," gave Sid the "Life's a Bitch" sweatshirt, and vowed to go on a hunger strike.

The day the Kendricks family moved, Debbie promised to call Sid from every rest stop between Detroit and Romance, Nevada. She called three hours later from a gas station in Kalamazoo. "I love you," she sobbed, "and I know Dad will send me back to Detroit when he sees me wasting away like this." Two hours later she called from a rest stop outside Chicago. She wasn't crying anymore. "I'm starving to death," she complained, "but at least I've got our love to comfort me." A few more hours passed, and Debbie called from a Burger King in Des Moines, Iowa. "I've got to quit calling you," she said around bites of a Whopper with cheese, "or I'll be broke before I even get to Romance."

True, it was good to hear Debbie feeling positive again, but it depressed the hell out of Sid. For years he'd depended on her up attitude to lift *him* up with her. With Debbie, anything was possible.

Without Debbie, Sid stands in the middle of the kitchen linoleum, afraid that a neighbor might see him in the backyard wearing Mom's shiny red boots. A Debbie voice in his head says, "And the neighbor could be color-blind! Sid, remember, things are seldom—"

"—what they seem," he says aloud, and tiptoes

outside in Mom's boots, where he immediately meets Mrs. Weston, the next-door neighbor. She is not color-blind.

"Hello, Mrs. Weston."

"Happy New Year, Sid." She is throwing rock salt onto her driveway.

"Happy New Year." He can feel her eyes staring at the red plastic. "Well . . . I suppose you're wondering why I'm wearing red boots," he says, adding a little "heh, heh" on the end of the sentence while he tries—desperately—to think of a "funny" reason he might be wearing them.

"Not at all," she says, tossing salt. "You're probably wearing them for the same reason I'm wearing my husband's."

He looks down and sees a pair of cloddy black boots (just like the ones Sid usually wears) on her feet. Sid smiles to himself as he makes his way across the thin layer of snow and begins tossing fruitcake onto the lawn. Then he begins pondering the possible reasons why Mrs. Weston *might* be wearing her husband's boots. She interrupts this train of thought. "Taking over for your mother, I see," she says. "I mean, feeding the birds."

"Well, she's on a date tonight."

"So's Jeremy." Jeremy Weston is Sid's age; they used to be good friends B.D. (before Debbie), but they don't hang out too much lately. "What about you, Sid?"

Sid is busy thinking that he should try to renew his

friendship with Jeremy. He doesn't really hear the question until she repeats it. "Aren't you going out for New Year's, Sid?"

"Well, no," he says. "My girlfriend moved away, and—"

"But didn't she move away *months* ago? Your mother told me she moved two or three months ago. Why, Jeremy has had two or three girlfriends since school started!"

He squeezes a piece of fruitcake between his fingers. Finally he says, "I think this is a little different."

"How so?" She asks it in that offhand way that means she's dying for the explanation. He knows his story will be all over the neighborhood by morning . . . but he really needs to talk.

"Because we were going together for over two years!" he says. "We didn't split up on our own. We were pulled apart. Separated! It's not *fair* that things like that can happen to two people!"

"Maybe not. . . . But think about how things were when your father died."

For one tenth of a second Sid gets the same weird feeling in his stomach he always gets when someone says those words: "your father." Actually Sid can't remember back to when he was three and his father died. But from the back of his mind he pulls out a memory of a man—presumably his dad—with scratchy cheeks and a rumbling voice who tossed him in the air. Sid knows he's missed something, but he's not sure what. He only feels it when he sees some father and son up at Baskin-Robbins or driving by in a car. He only feels it when someone says those words: "your father."

"Well, Mrs. Weston," Sid says, choosing his words carefully, "this is a whole different thing with Debbie. I mean, I can barely remember my dad, so to compare losing Debbie—"

Mrs. Weston says, "I'm not talking about when *you* lost your father. I'm talking about your mother. When she lost her husband."

"Oh." He dumps the rest of the fruitcake onto the lawn, then stands looking at the cold sky. Rain is beginning to spatter the snow.

"I'm getting soaked," says Mrs. Weston. "Do you want to come in for some hot chocolate, Sid?"

He continues to stare into the sky. "No, thank you."

"Well, have a happy New Year then, Sid. Come over to see Jeremy sometime."

"Okay."

Sid walks back to the house slowly, and steps out of the red boots. He wonders about his mother. Not as Mom. Not as Mrs. Linwood, the restaurant manager. But as Gloria Linwood, real person. He's not sure he knows her. Not once in all the years has she ever told Sid how she felt when his father died. She usually acts happy—even *goofy*. But how does she really feel?

A few months ago, when Sid got a part-time job, his mother said, "Oh boy, do I remember going to apply for my first job. I was twenty-eight years old and had never supported myself in my life. Walking in and applying for that waitress job was the hardest thing I'd ever done." But she never did say anything about the fact that she was twenty-eight when her husband died or that she had a baby to support.

Sid wants to slap himself for never asking.

But thinking back to her story, he doesn't really feel sad for her. It makes him feel good to know she survived. He thinks he will too.

Sid turns on the radio and his feet move to the music as he removes the ornaments from the tree (breaking only one) and wraps them in tissue paper. The candles come down from the mantel; cards are untaped from the wall and stacked on his mother's desk. He puts on the red boots once more in order to drag the Christmas tree down to the curb. It's raining harder now, and a frozen glaze is forming on the snow.

Sid hears shouts and bells, horns and firecrackers. It's midnight. He remembers kissing Debbie at midnight one year ago, but it doesn't hurt to think about it; it just seems like a nice memory. It's a Detroit custom to shoot off guns to mark the New Year, so he hurries from the street, pausing at the doorway to join in the noise by raising his voice in one loud shout.

A few minutes later he sits down at his desk in front of a clean pad of paper. Without even thinking, he writes, "Dear Debbie—" He stares at the page for twenty seconds before he can decide on the next word: "Tonight." But he doesn't know exactly what he wants to say. Tonight I took down the Christmas tree? Tonight I fed the birds last year's fruitcake? Tonight I was talking to my next-door neighbor? He crosses out "Tonight" and begins again: "Tomorrow." And the letter turns into a bunch of scribbled notes about all the things he plans to do this coming year. Talk to Mom more. Visit the long-neglected Jeremy Weston. Sign up for the chess club. (Learn how to play chess first.) Get to know Julie Judson, who sits across from him in English.

Sid remembers seeing an ad for a photography class at the local community college. Isn't it true that up until the time he met Debbie, his principle goal in life was to become a photographer for *Playboy* magazine? Debbie had talked him out of that career ("Sexist!" she'd shouted over and over), but he still enjoyed fooling around with a camera. He liked to take pictures of his mother working in her garden (although she always waved him away) and pictures of the birds that came daily to the Linwood backyard Triscuit–ham-bone–peach-pie–moldy-cheese feasts.

He grabs the community-college brochure but is momentarily defeated to see that you must be eighteen to take the course. Then he decides he'll pass himself off for eighteen by growing a mustache. Of course, by the time he can grow a real mustache, he probably *will* be eighteen! Sid laughs, and realizes he hasn't heard himself laugh for a long time.

He looks at the clock: one forty-eight A.M. For over an hour and a half he has thought about the future without sighing. For over an hour and a half he has felt good about life. For over an hour and a half he has not thought about Debbie Kendricks.

The front door opens. "Sidney!" his mother calls from the hallway. Uh-oh. The name "Sidney" is used only when (on a scale of one to ten) Mom's emotions are running at least a six or a seven. "Sidney Linwood!" she yells. That's even worse: She adds the "Linwood" only if she's at a nine.

He slides down the stairs in his socks, still holding a bunch of papers in his hand. When he sees Mom and Dickie embracing under the mistletoe (very embarrassing), he realizes it's the only decoration he has forgotten to take down. The weird thing is that Mom is still wearing her coat and gloves. She comes running toward Sid and hugs him. "Happy New Year, sweetheart!"

"Happy New Year," says Sid, realizing he *is* happy.

"Honey, would you help me get out of these things?" she says.

"Huh?"

"Would you help me take off my coat and . . . gloves?"

"Are you sick, Mom?"

"No." She begins to look a little impatient. "Look, Sid, just take off my gloves, okay?"

"Okay," says Sid, beginning to wonder how many

times she and Dickie have toasted in the New Year. He pulls off her right glove. He pulls off her left glove. "Here," he says, handing her the gloves.

"Sid," she says, and stares down at her left hand.

"What, Mom?"

"Sid," she repeats, and she twists her hand back and forth to catch the hallway light.

"Mom, why do you keep saying my name?"

"Sidney Linwood, would you please look down at the third finger on my left hand and tell me what you see!"

"A ring." He can't figure it out; Mom certainly has worn rings before . . . but never a diamond ring. Suddenly he realizes what it means. At least he thinks he does, but just in case he's wrong, he doesn't want to embarrass Dickie. "Is that like an engagement ring?" he asks hesitantly.

"Well, it's about time you figured it out," she says, slapping at him with her gloves.

For about thirty seconds all kinds of thoughts roller coaster through Sid's mind: Mom's getting married! Dickie's gonna be my stepfather! Is he going to move in here, or will we move somewhere else? Aren't they a little old to— No, that's silly. He looks up at her face and sees the same kind of glow that Debbie used to have when they were alone together. "Well, Mom, that's great!" He hugs her. "Dickie, congratulations." He shakes Dickie's hand.

"Let me get a picture of this!" he says, running upstairs for his camera, and when he returns, Mom

85

has brought out ginger ale in three champagne glasses. She and Dickie pose with raised glasses. "To the future," says Mom. "To the future," says Dickie.

"To the future," says Sid, snapping the picture.

Later, the living room is illuminated only by the TV when Sid enters in his pajamas. His mother and Dickie aren't watching, really. Mostly they're just giving each other soulful glances. But that's okay. "Mom, I'm going to bed now. I just wanted to say good night. And congratulations again. Congratulations to you both."

His mother says, "Thank you, honey. And don't forget, we've got a date: January second, bright and early, at Sears—to buy you that Partridge Family sweatshirt!"

He is suddenly so overpowered by love for her that he comes behind the couch and hugs her.

"What a night!" she whispers, then kisses him on the cheek.

"What a night," he replies.

If only she knew.

And when he goes into his bedroom and sees the autographed picture of Debbie, he doesn't moan, or curse Mr. and Mrs. Kendricks, or carry the picture into bed with him. He just pauses at the dresser, looks at Debbie, and smiles. When you left, it seemed like the world was ending, he thinks, but it didn't. Debbie, in her silver frame, smiles back as if to say: Things are seldom what they seem.

He dreams there is a fire alarm at school. He puts down his pencil, gets up from his desk, and goes to the door as the alarm rings even louder. Then Sid wakes with a start. It's not a fire alarm. The phone is ringing. The ice-blue digital numbers on his clock radio say 3:01 A.M.

Three oh-one A.M.! Either it's a wrong number, or there's a family emergency. Frost begins to form on his aorta. He picks up the phone. "Hello?"

First there is the sound of a noisemaker—a whistling squeal, then a voice: "Happy New Year!"

"Happy wrong number," says Sid with relief and starts to hang up.

There is a squawking from the other end of the line. "No! No! Wait! Sid, wait!"

At the sound of his name, he jerks the phone to his ear again. The voice did say "Sid," didn't it? Could it be . . . possibly . . . ?

He twists his hand in the bedclothes and slowly says the word: "Debbie?"

"Of course it's Debbie! Happy New Year!"

Relief and anger still swirl inside his head, but for very different reasons now. She still likes me! She called! . . . But why the hell did she wait until three A.M.?

He tries to sound casual when he says, "Who did you spend New Year's with?"

"*You!* I'm spending it with you!"

"No, I mean at midnight."

"It *is* midnight!"

He suddenly remembers the three-hour time difference between Detroit and Romance, Nevada.

He feels happy . . . and a little sad. Happy that Debbie still cares, happy that she called, but sad because after tonight he knows things will never go back to the way they were before. He's got a photography class coming up, and Mom's wedding, and (why not?) maybe even the Spring Dance. And he has a feeling that after only four letters (five if you count the Christmas card) Debbie might be working on a future too. "Debbie! Listen, this has been a wild night in the life of Sid Linwood. . . ."

Sid's mother appears in his doorway. Outlined by the dim hallway light, she pulls her robe tighter. "Sid? Sid, dear? Did I hear the—?"

"Yeah, I'm on the phone."

"Is something wrong? It's not Dickie? . . ."

"No, everything's cool. It's Debbie."

"But it's so late. Doesn't she know it's three A.M.?"

"Things are seldom what they seem, Mom," says Sid. "It's not three A.M. It's three o'clock *midnight*!"

"I'll let you get back to your call," she says as she gently shuts his door.

The Substitute

Nothing was ever the same after that Thursday night. The radio played an old Carpenters song in Ann's kitchen as she wrestled with her mother's electric mixer. I sat at the table eating chocolate chips and admiring how the ceiling light made the top of Ann's dark-brown hair shine like melted butter.

I was a poet. Or thought I was.

"Jim, make sure you leave enough chips for the cookies," she said.

"Uh . . . sorrrry," I said, looking down at the empty Nestle's bag and trying not to smile.

"You're not sorry one bit and you know it!" She was also trying not to smile. "Well, now we have to go to the A&P."

Ann's determination to make cookies had already resulted in flour splotches on her cheekbones and the meltdown of her mother's favorite Tupperware spatula. A ten-minute trip to the store might be just the thing to help her unwind.

"Oh, let's not drive," she said when I pulled out the keys to my Corvette. "Let's walk."

I drew back the kitchen curtain so she could see the thornbush scratching at the wind. "It's a pretty wild night."

" 'Wild nights should be our luxury,' " she quoted.

We always talked like that. Emily Dickinson was our favorite poet.

In fact, Emily Dickinson had brought us together. During junior year we had each taken Honors English from Mrs. Morganstein. I had the class first hour, Ann had it fifth. Just by chance we both wrote our final term papers on Mrs. Morganstein's favorite poet. One day she invited us back after school to "talk Dickinson." At first I didn't think Ann and I were going to connect at all. I was smart, popular, and good-looking. Ann was smart. It took me a while to realize she didn't *need* to be popular. And although she wasn't pretty in the conventional sense, her beauty could sneak up on you. At the end of the hour, Ann was smiling, I was smiling, and Mrs. M. was smiling. . . . In addition to being the best teacher at Mendota High School, Mrs. Morganstein was a pretty gifted matchmaker.

Now, as seniors in Honors English, Ann and I sat across the aisle from each other, watching Mrs. Morganstein rush around the room, hands always in motion, a sweater sliding off her shoulders, as she reeled off references to Shakespeare and Robert Frost or Doonesbury and Peanuts. Every Friday was "treat day," meaning some member of the class would bring in cookies or cupcakes or brownies. That was the kind of class Mrs. Morganstein taught—and the reason we were running down the street that windy Thursday night to buy chocolate chips for Ann's "treat day" cookies. The wet pavement slid beneath our feet. Above us tall, bare oak branches seemed to reach up and toss the stars around. Ann pointed to the intersection ahead, where a police car flashed red lights in and out of puddles. At the curb people were gathered near two cars savagely wrapped around each other.

"Hey, that's an orange Maverick," said Ann. "Just like the one Mrs. Morganstein drives."

Then she grabbed my arm. "Oh, my God," she said. And we watched as they lifted a woman we both recognized onto a stretcher, her face deathly still, her eyes wide open.

We walked back to Ann's house without saying a word, as if not discussing it could mean it never happened. I drummed my hands on the kitchen table while Ann continued making cookies, substituting butterscotch bits for chocolate chips. But when the last pan was coming out of the oven, the radio newscaster reported that a serious accident had occurred in town that evening. One driver was in critical condition, the other—a local high-school teacher—was dead on arrival at Grace Memorial Hospital.

The next afternoon one of the home-economics teachers baby-sat our English class. She said to use the period for studying, but everyone wanted to talk about Mrs. Morganstein and where they'd been and what they'd been doing when they heard the news. The fact that Ann and I had been right there drew a lot of attention; it was hard to tell the story. Ann attempted to pass out the butterscotch cookies, but not many people were hungry—and those who did try them said they tasted funny.

After a while Ann stood up and began to read aloud. I don't think I ever loved her more than that afternoon, as she stood in front of the class, reading the words of Mrs. Morganstein's favorite poet in a shaky voice. It was our class's private eulogy, and I think even the home-ec teacher was impressed because she put down her crossword puzzle to hear Ann read:

> *"We never know how high we are*
> *Till we are asked to rise*
> *And then if we are true to plan*
> *Our statures touch the skies—"*

The funeral was Saturday. I sat near the back of the chapel with Ann, and neither of us cried, although some kids did. I stared numbly at the casket knowing that smooth, wooden box had nothing to do with Mrs. Morganstein.

Even on Monday afternoon, I somehow expected to see her dash through the door of the classroom.

"It's going to be terrible, isn't it?" said Ann, twisting into her seat across the aisle.

I nodded. "It doesn't seem real."

When the door of Mrs. Morganstein's room slammed shut, everyone jumped, as if a volt of electricity were passing through the entire class. A man in his late thirties stood at the desk and surveyed the classroom. The clotted strands of brown hair combed across his head were arranged to give the illusion he wasn't balding, but that didn't stop his scalp from shining like the moon under the fluorescent lights. He had a sarcastic half smile on his face. His eyes dropped down on the desk, and he picked up Mrs. Morganstein's volume of Dickinson, read the title, and tossed it aside with a little snort.

"My name is Eugene Trippman," he said, "and I'm going to be your substitute teacher. I understand that most of the honors courses at this school are designed with an open curriculum, so that you can waste both your time and the instructor's by dabbling away at poetry, plays, and artistic basket weaving."

"Wait a second," said Doreen Winston, without even raising her hand. "This is the hardest course I ever took."

"And what about the senior research paper?"

someone else asked. "Are you calling *that* easy?"

"Easy is a very subjective term," he said, looking around to make sure we all understood. "I don't believe in an open curriculum. I believe in hard work. I believe in the basics. I have an M.A. in English literature, and I taught college composition for almost ten years. Without even looking at your work, I think I can safely say there is not a single student in this classroom who can work on that level."

His tone was so superior, so patronizing, that I had to speak up. "Test us, then," I said.

He looked deep into me, then walked slowly toward my desk asking, "What is your name?"

It was the easiest question in the world, but the force of his voice, the way he almost stared *through* me, pushed the words right back down my throat. I finally said, "James O'Brien."

"Well, Mr. O'Brien," he said. "Since you seem so confident, we'll test you first. Tell me, what is a nonrestrictive appositive?"

I'd never heard the term before. It must have something to do with grammar, I thought. Everyone in the class had heard me rave on about becoming a great poet or novelist someday—would they laugh at me now? Did *they* know what it meant? After a few moments of total silence, I said, "Well, I'm sure if I saw an *example*, I'd know what it was—and how to use it in a sentence."

94

He raised his eyebrows. "Oh, is a nonrestrictive appositive something you use in a sentence?"

"Yes," I said, then: "It is, isn't it?"

"Not so sure, are you? You strike me as the type of young man who thinks he knows quite a lot. Am I right?"

There was no way to answer that question.

"Do you intend to go to college?" he continued.

"Notre Dame," I said. O'Briens had gone to Notre Dame for the last four generations.

"Oh I *see*," he said sarcastically. "Honors student?" I nodded. "Captain of the football team?"

"No, I play baseball. And I'm not the captain."

"But you are . . . ah, let's see . . . president of the senior class?"

"Vice," I admitted, wondering what to expect next.

"And a nice girlfriend and a nice new car, too, I suppose?"

"Corvette," someone in the back of the room muttered.

"All that and Notre Dame," he said. "Very nice. And you're sure you'll get into the school?"

Of course I was sure. But how would that sound? I sort of smiled and said, "Well . . . with any luck."

"In *my* classes we don't deal in luck. We deal in basics. Like nonrestrictive appositives. Remember that."

He turned away and moved up and down the

95

aisles, discussing the new curriculum and picking on a lot of kids. I could barely hear him because of the ringing in my ears. The way he cataloged my accomplishments had somehow turned them into character flaws.

When the bell rang, there was a collective sigh of relief as we all rushed from the room. Ann grabbed my arm. "What are we going to do?" she asked. I shrugged because I didn't trust my voice to say anything out loud. She reached into her purse and pressed something into my hand. "He doesn't deserve to have this in his classroom," she said, then hurried off to the chem lab.

In my hand was Mrs. Morganstein's leather-bound *The Poems of Emily Dickinson.*

I kept the book at home on my desk and meant to return it to the classroom as soon as the substitute left and a permanent replacement took over. But two weeks later Mr. Trippman announced he would be filling the position for good. I never returned the book. By then we were enemies. There were others in the class he seemed to dislike, but none more than me. I always left his class with a pain in my stomach.

"I think we should report him to the principal," Ann said. "He's picking on you!"

"Oh, Dr. Doby, the new teacher's *picking on me*!" I said in a whiny voice, but as soon as I saw the hurt look on Ann's face, I was sorry I said it. "Look," I explained. "What can I really report? He's not saying all that much. He's crafty. It's the tone of his voice—sarcastic—the way he looks at me . . . I don't know."

"What about Walt Whitman?" said Ann.

I felt a white-hot flash of anger at the mention of that poet. A week before, Trippman happened to notice a book on my desk and—right in the middle of class—reached over and picked it up. "Walt Whitman. One of our most infamous poets." He paused and looked at me. "Always a favorite of sexually confused youth." That was all he said, but I knew I'd never be able to read those poems again.

"Don't mention Walt Whitman anymore," I said to Ann.

"Then what about the time he made you redo all your homework?"

He'd claimed it was because of my messy penmanship—but Mrs. Morganstein had never complained much about my handwriting. Was it worth going to the principal about? Other kids lived through teacher problems. How would it look if I went running to Dr. Doby the first time I had trouble?

I tried to explain this to Ann, but she just got angry. "If you aren't going to defend yourself, *who is*?" she demanded. "*I* can't! It's bad enough for me in there. And the rest of the kids—I think a lot of them are glad to see you fall; you've had everything going for you for so long. They're jealous."

"No, they aren't," I said. But even as I said it, it began to make sense. Lately there were little giggles from the back of the room each time Mr. Trippman started in on me.

For the next two months we plowed through "basics." Grammar, punctuation, spelling. Despite all the writing we did, we'd never actually sat down and *learned* the material before. Now, having to apply names to these concepts, to memorize, to be *tested*, made me feel I was running after something I couldn't quite catch—no matter how hard I tried. He knew how hard I was working, yet he'd always say the same thing to me in a loud singsong voice: *"You're not trying!"* He gave the exact opposite advice to Ann. One day as she struggled into her seat, she dropped her pencils and pens all over the floor. Being Ann, she carried a lot of pencils and pens. And being Ann, it seemed to take forever for her to pick them all up. "Ann," said Mr. Trippman, "you try too hard. Take it easy."

Right before my eyes, Ann slowed down, smiled, and picked up the pencils very casually—when ten seconds before it had been like watching her try to pick up drops of mercury. He smiled down at her. "Life's too short. Save yourself for the big things."

That afternoon, as we drove home from school in a snowstorm, I bitterly repeated, " 'Save yourself for the *big things*.' Like that big red C on your next report card."

Ann just stared out the window. It was report-card day, and my final grade for the semester was a C. The first C I ever received in my life—saved from a

D only because the A's Mrs. Morganstein had given me earlier in the semester were averaged in with Trippman's grades. "I know one thing," I said. "If Mrs. Morganstein were here, I'd have an A on that report card."

"I would too," she said, and turned red. It was the first B she'd ever gotten. "But, Jim—I've been thinking about this for a while now: Do you think Mrs. Morganstein was really a good teacher?"

"The best. The absolute best. How can you even ask that? We got to write poetry, and stories—and you won that Scholastic Prize for your essay last year."

"I know, but—"

"And she loved to talk about literature, and talk about—"

"Yes, she loved to talk. So we talked and ate chocolate-chip cookies, and it was really fun, but we never learned grammar or any of the things Mr. Trippman says we need to know for college. And now it's hard for us to catch up. I know, it's an *honors* class—whatever that means—but I'm beginning to think I know even less than the kids in the regular English classes."

"*I'm* beginning to think he's just trying to keep me out of Notre Dame."

"Would that be such a tragedy—not getting into Notre Dame?"

I turned and stared at her.

"You're so hung up on Notre Dame, but is it the

education itself that's important, James, or just the idea of going to *Notre Dame*?"

"I can't believe you said that." I turned the corner so fast, the Corvette slid into the curb. "You know how I feel about education: I've been an honors student since I was born."

"Right. And now that things are harder, you can't take it. Face facts. How much time have you spent studying for Trippman's class compared to how much time you spend complaining about him?"

"You *know* he's gone out of his way to harass me. But why? Why me?"

"I don't know. Does it really make any difference? The point is, are you going to let him get to you— or are you going to try to make the best of it?" The cold air turned her words into little clouds floating in the air between us.

Does it really make any difference? It made all the difference in the world to me, and if she couldn't see it, there was something really wrong. As I pulled into her driveway, I said, "I can't make it tonight for studying."

She bent her head and began to rub her hands together as if they were freezing. "Okay," she said quietly.

"Or tomorrow night either."

She looked up at me. For a moment we just stared at each other. She looked so hurt. I wanted to grab her hand, I wanted to quote Emily Dickinson. *And*

I wanted her to be on my side against Trippman!
But then she softly said, "Fine then. Don't come
over, Jim," and climbed out of the car, walking away
through the falling snow.

The next semester, we still had the same seats in
Honors English, but the aisle between us could have
been a mile wide. After Christmas, Trippman told us
we would begin to study literature and writing again.
He said: "Now that you know the basics . . . well,
now that *most* of you" (this with a pointed look in
my direction) "know the basics, it's time to move on
and see how they apply in your own writing."

I worked for a whole week on the poem I submit-
ted, throwing away page after page of paper as I read
each draft through Mr. Trippman's prejudiced eyes.
My hand was shaking when I finally turned it in.
Several days later Trippman stood in front of the
class with our graded assignments. "Some of them
were good, and some of them . . . well, you'd just
have to read them to believe them." He rolled his
eyes and the class laughed. "So I'm going to share
a couple of these papers with you," he said. And
then he began to read my poem:

"The leaf was on the tree.
It fell,
it dropped,
it died.

I embrace the trunk
and trace the limb,
then touch the twig
that lost the leaf.
My hand is lifted toward the sky.
But my fingers are not large enough.
Or bold enough or old enough.
Or bright enough or right enough.
To be the leaf. Though I try—
Too dim, too small.
Twisting, searching for the sun,
Waiting for the fall.''

Was it the fact that he moaned "Oh, God" after the first line, or was it the eyeball rolling and sarcastic voice that made me suddenly hate the poem too? By the time he finished reading, the whole class was in hysterics. His eyes roved up and down the aisles, connecting with other eyes as if sharing a private joke. But his eyes did not meet mine until he said, "That little masterpiece was created by our poet laureate, Mr. O'Brien." It wasn't just my imagination that the laughter increased at that point. Without meaning to, I looked over at Ann. At least she wasn't laughing. But when the bell rang, she didn't come over to me either. She disappeared down the hall with Luke Bartell, and I wondered if I had imagined our whole relationship.

After class Doreen Winston caught up with me in

the hallway. "I just want you to know that Trippman did a terrible thing today." Before I could thank her, she had melted back into the crowd.

It happened many times. Trippman almost always read my papers aloud. For some reason I always expected Ann to come up to me after class on those afternoons, though she never did. But Doreen almost always appeared in the hallway to say how unfair it was. I thought of asking her to the Spring Dance, but then I started to wonder why, if Doreen thought my papers were so good, she never told Trippman that in class?

At the next marking period I forged my father's name on my report card for the first time. I was spending so much time preparing for Honors English that my other grades were falling as well. Where I usually got all A's and a B or two, I now had an unhealthy mixture of B's and C's. Of course, I got a D in English.

I wondered how much senior grades counted at Notre Dame.

The day after report cards, the coach called me into his office. I'd just pitched a 7–2 game—my first win that year. He motioned me to sit down, then told me I was off the team until my grades improved. *"Off the team?"* I jumped up. "You can't do this to me!"

"Wanna bet?" Nothing ever fazed Coach Higgs. When he started to pull out rule books and school policies regarding sports and academics, I knew I was defeated and walked back to the Corvette knowing, for the first time in my life, what it felt like to be a loser. Even the low, gray sky seemed to press me down, shrink me into nothingness.

The next day in class Trippman casually asked me, "How's baseball?"

No one laughed; no one knew I was off the team. But they must have known something was up, because it just wasn't his style to make idle chitchat with a student—especially me. "How's baseball?" he asked the next day and the next, and as more people learned I was off the team, he began getting some laughs. On the fourth day I decided I'd walk out when he asked me that question . . . but of course he never asked me again. He was smart that way. He'd take me right to the breaking point with something, then drop it before I exploded.

With all the free time I now had, I decided to put a real effort into the senior research paper. As a sort of tribute to Mrs. Morganstein, I chose to write on Emily Dickinson again, this time focusing on the topic of death. It gave me a lot of pleasure to use the leather-bound volume, and most nights I worked until I slumped over my desk. Once I dreamed that Trippman returned the paper to me with a big A+ on it, and I went bounding down the hallway like an astronaut walking on the moon. I bounced out of the school, jumping nine or ten feet in the air, arms reaching for the sky—then suddenly woke up, drooling on the leather-bound book, my eyes less than an inch from the dark print:

> *The Dying, is a trifle, past,*
> *But living, this include*
> *The dying multifold—without*
> *The Respite to be dead.*

"Yes," I said out loud. "Oh, yeah!" And when the time came to hand our research papers in, I had worked for over one hundred and twenty hours on mine.

All around me people were getting ready for graduation. I heard Ann was going to the prom with Luke Bartell. I wasn't going at all. Before Ann, I'd had no trouble getting a girlfriend. Now I was afraid to even ask a girl out. Because of my grades and my cut from the team, the rumor was circulating that I might be on drugs. No one understood.

I kept telling myself that things would change. It was too late for high school to improve, but I looked past graduation, beyond summer vacation, to the fall when I would be at Notre Dame. Things would change in the fall.

To prolong the agony, Trippman waited until the end of the last Honors English class to return our research papers. He handed them back, facedown, one by one. The students left the classroom still holding their papers down, as if afraid to peek at the grade. But from the hall I heard an occasional "Hallelujah" or moan. I realized there were only a handful of students left in the room. Then only five, then three, and then just one. Me.

The substitute and I were alone in Mrs. Morganstein's classroom, and he held out my paper, facedown.

And then he smiled.

I had the strangest feeling then. I felt as if he and I were very close; as if I were about to learn the secret to the bizarre game he'd been playing all year. I almost smiled back.

"As you may have guessed, I handed these papers back in order," he said. "From the highest to the lowest."

The smile I'd felt inside began to shrivel and die. I tried to move my mouth. Finally: "And I got the lowest grade in the class." It was more a statement than a question.

He nodded.

I took the paper from him, then walked toward the door. I was close to hitting him; I was close to tears. I turned around in the doorway and said, "Why?"

He looked at me blankly. "Why what? Express yourself clearly, in complete sentences."

"Why, all year, have you been against me? Why hasn't anything I've done been good enough?"

"I haven't been against you," he said. "And the last question you'll have to ask yourself: Why *wasn't* anything you did good enough?"

Then I slowly turned the paper over. On the first page, next to my thesis statement of ". . . and throughout her poetry Dickinson proves again and again one simple truth: the pain of living can hurt more than dying," he had written in red ink, "How would <u>you</u> know how dying feels? You are not dead." My fingers curled into fists.

Red ink covered each page. Paragraphs were crossed out, comments were begun in margins then arrowed around to cover the back side of the page. Phrases like "repetitive," "boring," "bad construction," and "grammar!" seemed to fly off the page and sear themselves into my eyes. On the last page was a big red D— and, in print at least an inch tall, "TOTALLY INSUFFICIENT WORK!" The words blurred, and I crumpled the paper, slamming it to the floor. He was still smiling, and now I could see that the smile was one of satisfaction. "God damn you," I said, then ran out the door, knowing that if I stayed in his presence for even one second more, *he* would know how dying felt because I would kill him.

I never did go to Notre Dame. All my grades had suffered that horrible year, and my final grade of D in Honors English was the killing blow for a prospective English major. After the first rejection from Notre Dame, my father pulled some strings and arranged a private conference with a dean. I'm not sure what I said to the dean at the meeting. I remember that he looked a lot like Mr. Trippman. I think mostly I just stared at him. Two weeks later I got the second rejection. I ended up at Michigan State University, majoring in English as planned, but I could never feel quite the same about school, English, or even myself. I did have a couple of poems published in the college literary magazine, but they weren't very good and I blamed Mr. Trippman. It got to the point where I blamed him for *everything*—as if I couldn't tell where his influence ended and my life began.

When I took the job teaching English, I told myself I'd only work until my first book was published, but after eight years I was still grading papers and erasing blackboards. Occasionally I saw students in my classes who reminded me of myself as a teenager: too confident, too popular, too happy. I wanted to tell them something, but I wasn't sure what. This semester there was one boy in particular. He came into class the first day with a pretty girl on his arm and a letter on his sweater. He was loud; he was arrogant. I began my annual speech telling the students how difficult my course would be, how hard they would have to work. He raised his hand to remind me that this *was* an honors class *after all*, and they wouldn't expect anything less. I stared at him for a long time.

Then I slowly walked toward him and asked him his name.

Being Alive

Every Tuesday and Thursday afternoon the kid they called Kenny Wheels would come to watch our aerobics class. He'd sit against the wall, his face broken in half by a big smile, his fists banging double-time on the tray in front of him. Some people said he came just to watch the girls. It didn't matter to me; I wasn't particularly shy. And in a gym filled with girls in size-two pink, yellow, and orange leotards, I doubted he was paying much attention to a size twelve in a navy-blue sweatsuit like me. Besides, I was too busy with my own huffing and puffing to watch Kenny Wells in his wheelchair.

Until the day Kenny was kicked out of the gym.

Ms. Blair had just told us to pick up our jump ropes for the "aeropics" segment of the workout. A home-ec teacher by day, an exercise fiend by night, Ms. Blair was only a few years older than us seniors—but

considered very sophisticated because she was ru-
mored to have a live-in boyfriend. She claimed to
have invented aeropics, and all the girls were so
hung up on her that nobody questioned it. All I knew
was that it was the hardest part of the workout, and
the only reason I persisted at it was to burn up
enough calories to justify buying a Moon Pie or pack
of Twinkies on the way home without feeling guilty.

The music Ms. Blair played for the rope segment
was especially irritating. It started off nice and slow,
hop and pause and hop and pause, but steadily ac-
celerated to hop-hop-hop-hop-hop. By the time the
song ended, most of the girls were on the floor,
gasping. That particular day, two girls didn't stop
jumping when the song ended: Kathi Weiss and
Addie Haines. All through school Kathi had three
things working for her: She was very pretty, very
athletic, and had a name ending with *i*. Addie was
also pretty and could run like the wind, but she had
so much pride that if you threw a fifty-dollar bill at
her feet, she wouldn't stoop to pick it up. It probably
had something to do with the fact she was the only
black girl at our entire high school.

Addie and Kathi were longtime rivals. For three
years Addie had beaten Kathi in the girls' division of
our school's 3-K Funrun. There was always some
type of competition going on between them. That
afternoon they continued jumping rope, facing each
other, going faster and faster, until I wasn't sure their

feet were even hitting the floor. Everyone was cheering, urging them on. When Kathi finally fell out of rhythm and tumbled to the floor, everyone laughed. Everyone including Kenny, whose laugh was loud and wheezy. Addie was too proud to even crack a smile over her victory; she just reached out a hand to help Kathi get up. But Kathi got up on her own, her face red and sweaty. She listened to the laughter, then whirled at Kenny. "Stop that!" she shrieked. "Stop that horrible laughing!"

He tried to stop, but the laugh kept burbling out of his chest.

"What are you doing here anyway?" Kathi shouted. "This class is for *girls only*! Ms. Blair, make him leave! He's disrupting . . . everything!"

"Oh, Kathi . . ." Ms. Blair began, then shrugged.

"I mean it! I mean it!" Kathi shouted, stamping her foot. I remembered Kathi's eleventh-birthday party when she threw the same kind of tantrum because she didn't win at pin the tail on the donkey.

Ms. Blair shrugged again, twisting the chains at her neck. "Well, maybe you're right, Kathi. I guess we should be a little more businesslike in this class. Maybe we shouldn't allow visitors. Kenny—"

But she didn't have to finish the sentence, because he was already rolling toward the door with his head down, the thumb of his right hand controlling the button on his electric wheelchair.

When Addie followed him across the gym, I

thought she was just going to help him with the door. But she followed him right through it. "Addie? Addie, where are you going?" Ms. Blair called.

She came back and stood in the doorway, her thin brown arms folded across the front of her blue leotard. "I don't like discrimination, Ms. Blair. If we're not allowing people with handicaps in the gym today, I'm going outside to run the track."

"Discrimination? Handicaps? Addie, I'm not asking Kenny to leave because of— I'm asking him to leave because he's a boy, and this is an all-girls class."

Addie never looked away from Ms. Blair. "You didn't say anything when Mel Jacobs and the guys from the football team came in last week."

"But—"

"I don't want to hear any *buts*!" Addie Haines was the only person in the whole school who could get away with that kind of talk. "Okay, boys in wheelchairs aren't allowed today. Next week it might be black girls." She pointed to herself. "Or girls with blond hair." She pointed at Kathi. "Girls with sweatsuits." She pointed at me.

Then she walked out.

An hour later, when I left the gym, Addie was still running the outdoor track. She wasn't the only one out there, but she was definitely the fastest. I didn't realize Kenny was sitting under a tree until I heard him calling out, "Go! Go! Go!"

I said, "Kenny, I'm sorry about what happened in there."

He was leaning forward in his chair, following Addie's progress with his eyes. He shrugged. "Blair says— she invented— that aeropicise. What a liar." As always, he spoke with a lot of difficulty, twisting his head as if he were biting the words out of the air.

"Blair's a bitch," I said.

He laughed and clapped his hands over his mouth. His hands reminded me of lobster claws. The fingers on each hand all seemed to be glued together; his thumbs moved independently.

Addie raced by and raised a hand in greeting. "Go! Go! Go!" yelled Kenny.

"You like sports, huh?"

"Watching. Not really— participating," he said. He was a little guy, but for some reason he had a large, round face, and when he smiled—like he did at that moment—he looked like a happy jack-o'-lantern. "Aerobics," he said. "This is— my— aerobics." He lifted his hand and bent his thumb up and down several times. "Whew. Tired." He wiped imaginary sweat from his forehead with the side of his arm.

Addie ran off the track and sat down on the grass. "How's that?" she asked Kenny.

"Super!"

"Listen, Addie," I said, touching her arm. She leaned forward to tie her shoe—her way of pulling away without making a big deal of it. "That was a neat thing you did. I wish I'd had the nerve to walk out like that."

"You could have," she said, then turned to Kenny: "Thanks for pacing me like that."

He smiled.

"It worked," she said. "I ought to hire you as my trainer for the Funrun."

"What's it— like?" he asked.

"Winning?"

"No. Running."

Resting her chin on her knee, Addie looked off at the track.

When she didn't answer, Kenny said, "I wonder— because I don't— run. Can't find— Adidas— to fit my— wheels."

Addie smiled, but continued staring off. Finally she said, "When you start off, it feels like God's hand is on your back, giving you that first push. And then you're alone. It feels like you're part of the air. You're running *toward* something. . . ." Her voice trailed off and she shrugged. "When I'm running, it feels the way being alive *should* feel." She looked at Kenny and added, "At least, it does for me."

She immediately got up and began doing stretching exercises. Maybe she was a little embarrassed. But I wasn't. Because when she talked about running, for a moment I felt like I could run too. Kenny must have felt the same way, because he said, "I— want to feel it."

She was bent over, her right hand holding her left foot. She stayed that way for a moment. "Feel what, Kenny?"

"Like I'm part of the air."

"Okay," she said. "Let's go for a run."

She moved behind his chair and grasped the handles, but when she tried pushing, the wheels only moved a few feet. "How much does this thing weigh?"

"A lot," he said. "My chair— weighs— more than— I do."

I remembered back to when I was a sophomore and Kenny had just started attending our school. He used to wheel himself around on a nonmotorized chair. "Didn't you have another chair?" I said. "Before you got this one?"

"Antique," he said. "From when— I could use— my hands a lot."

"That would be easier to push," I said.

Addie said, "I'll tell you what, Kenny. Some night we'll come to the track with your other chair. I'll take you for a ride so fast your wheels will spark."

He bounced up in his seat. "Tonight?"

"Where are you going, Nancy?" my younger sister asked that evening. My sister was a Kathi-Weiss-in-training, resembling Kathi in everything from her clothes and hairstyle to her stubborn refusal to call me "Nance." Nance was plain. It was me: Nance Sherman. Nancy sounded too much like Micki,

Muffy, Buffy, and all the other names the girls at our school were called.

"Out," I said, letting her draw her own conclusions.

"With a *boy*?"

"Maybe," I said, and left for the school yard.

Kenny's mother was to drop him at the high school at six thirty P.M. No one had invited me to join them, but I went anyway. I guess I just wanted to see how Kenny enjoyed "running."

"Nance!" Kenny shouted, waving a claw in my direction.

Addie didn't seem surprised to see me. She was bent over, attaching Kenny's belt to the back of the wheelchair. Then she straightened and pushed the chair over to the track. No one else was running, but the big floodlights were still turned on because the football team had just finished practicing. The light caught Addie in profile, making her look like a proud African princess. "How fast— will we be— running?" Kenny asked.

"Like the wind," said Addie, and took off.

The light danced over and through the wheels, making Spirograph designs on the track. Feet pounded and wheels whirred, and then I heard it: Kenny's voice yelling, "Wheee!" His excitement pushed Kenny's voice into the upper register. It was the most amazing sound I'd ever heard. And that word! I couldn't remember saying "Wheee!" even as a child, but to hear a sixteen-year-old boy shout it just about broke my heart.

As they came around the last corner, facing me, I could see Kenny's face was completely split by that huge grin. Addie's breath was coming in little puffs of vapor, but—as always—she looked cool and aloof. I thought they'd pull over when they made a complete circle, but Addie kept going, around and around the track until something strange happened. The lights were set to go off automatically at seven o'clock, and when they did, the track went pitch dark. I couldn't see them at all, but I could hear the wheels, the feet, the breathing, the "Wheee!" and suddenly I felt I was there with them, running through the dark. First I felt I was Kenny being propelled through the night; then I was Addie, pounding the ground and pushing the chair in front of me. And then I was part of the air. It lasted only a second— that feeling—but when Addie and Kenny finally came off the track, I felt as high as if I'd been running too. My heart was beating fast, I was taking deep gulps of air.

I could hear Kenny bouncing around in his chair, saying, "Super! Super! Super!"

In the dark we sat and talked. I asked Addie what made her start running. "What made me start breathing?" she replied. "I've always run, but I didn't get into competition until I got to this school. I guess I got tired of being an outcast."

"You're not an outcast!" I said, thinking cliques and social circles were the last thing Addie seemed interested in; she always seemed above that sort of thing. "Now if you want to talk about outcasts, let's talk about *me*. I've never fit into anything in my life—including my Levi's."

Addie said, "I started entering the races to show them that I may act like an outcast and look like an outcast, but, hey, I've got it!"

"It?" said Kenny.

"It!" she said. "Whatever it takes to beat them. I'm showing them it's okay to be different."

"Outcasts, outcasts," said Kenny. "Am I the— only one here— who's always been an— average, normal guy?"

I wasn't sure how to take that until he started laughing. Then I laughed too. Addie's laugh was soft and low. I'd never heard her laugh before.

Kenny turned to me. "Don't you— run, Nance?"

"Only after Good Humor trucks," I said. "I mean, can you see this body in a race?"

"Why not?" said Addie.

"My sister calls me the Sherman tank," I said.

"I wish— I could run," said Kenny.

"You just did," said Addie.

"In a race," he said. "Run— in a race."

There was a long moment of silence. Then she said: "You can. You can run in a race. With me." It was too dark to see the expression on Addie's face.

But I've always wondered what she looked like when she said those words.

The next day I approached her at school. "You aren't serious about running with Kenny in the Funrun."

"I am."

"Don't get me wrong," I said. "It's nice and all that, but it also means you're going to *lose.*"

"Winning doesn't make that much difference to me," she said. "Running does."

"But, Addie, they do have sports events for the handicapped. Maybe he could get into that sometime."

"No," she said forcefully. "He wants to feel like everyone else at this school, and I'm going to help him do it."

I said, "You don't have to run for him just because he can't."

"I'm not doing it *because he can't,*" she said. "I'm doing it *because I can.*"

"Because I can": That must have been Addie's motto. I remembered the first time I heard her say that, the year we were freshmen. Addie had just won her first Funrun, and Kathi—who had lost by fifty seconds—went up to congratulate her. She pressed her cheek against Addie's, but her eyes were burning with anger. Later, walking away from the awards stand, I heard Kathi say in her most patronizing voice, "Well, Addie, I guess you run because you're trying for a sports scholarship to college, right?"

Addie turned cold eyes upon her. "No. My father is a pediatrician, so I guess he can afford to send me just about anyplace I want to go." Kathi's mouth dropped open just a millimeter, and Addie stared at her. "Why do *you* run, Kathi?"

Kathi shrugged. "Because I'm good at it, I guess. Because I think I can win."

"Ah," said Addie, holding a long, dark finger in front of Kathi's nose. "You run because you want to win. I run because I can."

At the time I didn't understand what she meant—that she could run just for the joy of it. I knew how I'd feel if I ran: I'd want the awards. Even now I found it hard to believe Addie could pass up the chance to win.

I said, "But Addie, you're a senior. This will be your last chance for the Funrun. You won't be here next year."

She looked past me. "Kenny may not be here next year either."

"What do you mean? He's only a junior."

"I mean that I've been looking at some of my father's medical books," she said.

"I don't want to hear this," I said.

"Remember when he could talk more clearly than he does now? When he could wheel himself around in his chair? When he could move his fingers and take notes in class instead of carrying around that big tape recorder?"

"Don't tell me any more," I said, walking away.

I was always walking away from things I didn't want to hear. My father liked to tell about the time I was three years old and they brought my little sister home from the hospital. I hid under the bed, yelling, "Is it gone yet?" Maybe I hadn't changed much.

That night I ended up at the school yard. I knew I would. Again nobody had asked me to come.

Addie wheeled Kenny out to the track. "Keep your eye on the stopwatch," she told him.

"I can do that," I said.

"I'll keep you— going fast." He twisted his head around to look at her face. "I'll cheer— a lot."

"Sounds good," she said, and took off running.

"Go! Go! Go! Go!" I heard Kenny shout.

I watched the seconds tick around the stopwatch. When they came back, Addie said, "What was our time?"

I held up the watch, and she grimaced. "Well, usually I go about twice as fast as that," she muttered. "Let's try it again."

And that was how it went every night for the next three weeks. I'd leave the house—leaving my sister with the impression I was going on a date— and meet Addie and Kenny at the track. I'd hold the stopwatch as Addie ran and Kenny shouted encouragement. Sometimes I even felt like I was part of the air again.

Two nights before the race Addie ran the whole 3-K, just to make sure she could do it. She was wiped out when she got back, and their time wasn't that good. But it didn't seem to bother her. "We did it," she told Kenny. "We did run the whole three kilometers."

"We did it!" he shouted, and he looked happy, really happy.

Addie told us to meet her in front of the school at seven on Friday evening. For the first time she made a point of including me in the invitation. I thought she wanted me to time their last practice session, but when I got there, Addie was wearing a skirt instead of her usual leotard. "What's going on?" I asked. "Aren't you practicing tonight?"

"Not tonight," said Kenny.

Addie began pushing his chair down the sidewalk, and I ran to help her. "Where are we going?" I asked.

"Dinner," said Addie.

We walked the two blocks to a small restaurant I'd never noticed before. There were only a few people inside, all of them older than our parents. It was the type of restaurant most of the kids at our school would laugh at, but The Pasta Bowl—with its Italian songs on the jukebox and red plastic tablecloths—was my kind of place. People yelled their orders across the room and ran back and forth with trays of pizza and pitchers of beer.

I went to the counter for a pitcher of Coke, and when I returned, Addie was saying, "It's a good idea to load up on a lot of carbohydrates the night before a race. I usually eat spaghetti, but some people like pizza or pancakes."

"Oh, boy," said Kenny. "I want a pizza."

"This is great," I said. "Next time my sister complains about my eating, I'm going to tell her I'm carbohydrate loading for a race."

Kenny tore open the end of his straw and blew the wrapper across the table at me; I shot mine back at him.

I realized it was the first time Addie, Kenny, and I had been together off the school track. All those nights we'd spent in training for the race were coming to an end. I didn't want to think about that. "Let's get a large pizza," I said.

Addie ordered a huge plate of spaghetti, and Kenny and I split the pizza. I sat there wolfing down my slices, and no one said, "Nancy, don't you think you've had enough?" or pushed salad at me. In fact, Addie offered me a taste of her spaghetti.

Kenny said, "Last year— when our homeroom won that prize— for best attendance— we had a pizza party." He paused to swipe at a strand of cheese hanging off his hand. "When I got my slice— Mrs. Pelton came over— and she wanted to— cut my pizza in small pieces."

"Why?" asked Addie.

"That's what I wonder," said Kenny. "She didn't want to cut— anyone else's."

I said, "That would make me really mad."

Kenny lowered his voice. "Pissed me off."

He reached forward with both hands and took another slice off the tray. "So when she was standing there beside my chair— I dropped my pizza. I dropped it right— on her skirt." He chewed for a few seconds, then added, "You know how sometimes— my hands don't work right." And he winked.

Addie and I burst out laughing, and Kenny joined in with his loud, wheezy laugh.

When it was time to leave, we all wanted to pay the check ourselves. Kenny took out his wallet and counted dollar bills while I tried to grab the check from Addie's hand. "No," said Addie. "I invited you two out."

"Okay," I said. "But next time I'm paying."

It wasn't until I was home in bed that I thought about what I'd said: "Next time." No one had ever said there'd be a next time.

The next morning I walked to the field in the early-morning cold. It was strange to see all the Kathis and Muffys and Phils and Chases of our town out on that track. For weeks it had been a private nighttime playground for Addie and Kenny and me.

When I finally found Addie and Kenny, they were in the middle of a confrontation with Kathi Weiss. "What do you think you're doing?" Kathi demanded.

"We're going to run," Addie replied calmly.

"Oh, no! Oh, no! You are *not* running with him."

"Try stopping us," said Addie.

"I just might! You better believe I just might! What is this, some hokey publicity stunt to get your name in the paper? Something to put on your college application?"

Kenny looked hurt for a second, and Addie moved in front of him—blocking Kathi from his view. "Listen, Weiss," she said. "Why don't you accept the fact that now you can win the girls' division—and just shut up."

Nobody ever told Kathi to shut up. She filled herself up with air to start yelling. But then a glimmer of understanding seemed to cross her face. She turned abruptly and walked away.

The race was almost ready to start. I only had time to say a quick "Good luck, you guys."

Addie smiled. Kenny stuck his thumb in the air.

"Runners, take your places," a voice boomed, and I ran off the track to stand in the crowd, never taking my eyes off them. His hands gripped the arms of the chair tightly. Her hands gripped the handles.

When the starting gun went off, seventy-two pairs of feet and one set of wheels went zipping across the line. The race course consisted of one lap around the track, then out onto the street for about a mile, and back to the track for another lap. Addie's legs were pumping like pistons, and the wheels of the chair spun so fast, I couldn't see the spokes. But by the time they had completed that first lap one thing was clear: They were going to lose.

Seeing Addie and Kenny about two thirds of the way behind the leaders, I knew there was no hope. Of course we'd known it all along, but I guess I still harbored some secret hope for a miracle. But now I could see Bob Beechum, Gary Rosen, and Perry Astor were shoulder to shoulder at the front of the pack. Of the girls, Kathi Weiss wasn't too far behind them. I had never seen so much concentration on her face.

When Addie and Kenny passed me and started out toward the street, neither of them looked in my direction. Addie was still pumping hard, and Kenny was yelling, "Go! Go! Go!"

I was used to Addie and Kenny's usual pace, where I could eat a big bag of Cheetos before they finished one kilometer. But this was different. It didn't seem all that long before the first runners were coming back into the field. I wondered how far behind my friends were. Perry Astor crossed the finish line, winning the boys' medal, and a few minutes later Kathi Weiss bounded across the line, tears of pain or exhaustion or happiness streaming down her face.

The announcer was calling off the finishes as each kid crossed the line. "Thirty-eight, thirty-nine, forty, forty-one."

And then I saw them coming back onto the track—Addie kicking her feet into the air, puffing like an engine, Kenny urging her on. When they finally crossed the finish line, Kenny's fists were raised in the air. They had come in forty-fifth. Addie walked the chair to a slow stop, then moved away as people gathered around Kenny, shaking his hand, patting his back. Occasionally, above their congratulations, I heard his voice: "Wow! Super! Super!"

And I realized it didn't matter to Kenny whether they came in first, forty-fifth, or seventy-second. He was happy just to be part of it. I went looking for Addie and found her standing near the stage, watching Kathi and Perry receive their medals. Addie stood tall—as always—and her head was held high—as always. But there was something in her eyes I'd never seen before.

"Hi!" I shouted, moving toward her. My first impulse was to hug Addie. But as I got closer, the look in her eyes told me to back off.

"Congratulations!" I said, standing in front of her, not sure what to do.

"Thanks," she said, then turned to watch the medal presentation.

"You did great!"

"Nance, please! I'm trying to watch the presentation."

I saw a hand go up to her eye and realized she was crying. Despite all her talk, winning *had* been important to her. It was kind of ironic, considering it didn't matter to Kenny at all. Then it hit me: The reason Addie had run with Kenny was that no one else would. Anyone else could have run with him—Kenny wouldn't have cared—while Addie ran for the medal. I said to Addie, "I never thought of this until now, but you should have been running. Someone else could have run with Kenny. *I* could have tried."

"Yes," she said coldly. "You *could* have."

For the next twenty-four hours I was miserable. I was furious at myself for being so dim-witted, so self-centered that I'd cost Addie her chance to win the race. I was furious at Addie for being such a hypocrite—saying she didn't care about winning when she really did. I was even mad at Kenny, because it seemed he was even more self-involved than I was. Didn't he realize Addie might have really wanted to run? Didn't he care that she was giving up her last chance just to give him a good time?

On Sunday evening I automatically put on my army jacket at six fifteen. I didn't realize I'd done it until my younger sister said, "Off to meet Mr. Right?" and I realized I'd been a hypocrite myself—deliberately trying to look good in my sister's eyes by inventing a boyfriend. I said, "I don't have a boyfriend. I never did. I'm going out to find my two friends, Addie Haines and Kenny Wells!"

. Then I crashed out the door. Behind me, my sister was shouting, "Kenny *Wheels*? The *cripple*? And that *black* girl?"

Of course, the field was dark, but I could hear her pounding footsteps on the track. I had never heard her run that fast before; I realized that all those weeks of pushing Kenny's chair had strengthened her, increased her speed. She ran for a long, long time, even though I was sure she knew I was there. Finally she came running off the track with a stop-watch in her hand and sat down beside me.

Now if she would only talk to me.

She held up the stopwatch and said, "My own private Funrun. I won. In fact, it was my best time ever." She didn't seem to be angry at me anymore.

I said, "Too bad I was the only one here to see it."

"Let's walk," she said, getting up.

We walked for a long time without talking. I think she was waiting for her breathing to level off before she spoke. Finally: "Yesterday was not one of my finer moments."

"Mine either," I admitted.

"I couldn't *believe* how bad it hurt to see Kathi Weiss with that medal around her neck. I couldn't *believe* how much I'd been lying to myself."

"I can't believe how dumb I've been," I said.

She continued, "I thought I was above that attitude, but I realized yesterday that I'm not. All yesterday and today I was down, down, down." Her voice dropped lower with each "down." "And then I thought to myself, Okay, Addie, so you're not perfect. You're petty and jealous and a hypocrite, so what? It's all part of being alive."

"I wish I could have that attitude," I began. "I can't stand myself."

"Neither can I sometimes," she admitted, and laughed.

We walked on in silence, heading for Kenny's house. We never said we were going there; we just did. And we ended up at the school a little while later, Addie on one side of the chair, me on the other, with Kenny between us, just taking a stroll down the track. Addie, Kenny, and me. Being alive.

The Attack of the Jolly
Green Giant

I want to have sex. As soon as possible.

But wanting and getting are two different things—everyone knows that. To illustrate: Last year, on my birthday, Ma asked what kind of presents I'd like. I wanted a personal computer, some videocassettes, and a ten-speed bike. I got a pair of pants, two shirts, and some underwear. Well, that's the difference between wanting and getting. I understand how it works—but it doesn't stop me from wanting.

Now my opinion is this: Every fifteen-year-old kid in the world has done it at least once. That's what all the guys at school say, that's what they say on TV, that's what they say in the magazines. It makes me feel like some kind of freak. Especially when you consider I start driver's ed this summer and haven't even kissed a girl yet! I once came close at Natalie Baskin's fourteenth-birthday party. We started this kissing game, and right when it was my turn to kiss Maxine Crowther, Mrs. Baskin came down the basement stairs, announcing, "Boys and girls, it's time for ice cream and cake!"

So I think it's time to start getting some experience . . . if only I could find someone to do it with. In the interest of finding that someone—and finding her fast—I've developed this simple four-question sex test. I'm just looking for someone who will answer "Yes!" to all four questions.

The David W. Ross Simple Four-Question Sex Test

1. Are you a girl?
2. Do you like to have fun?
3. Are you ready for a new experience?
4. Would you like to have sex with me?

So far I haven't had too much luck with the test. On the way to my first driver's-ed class, I decide to stop and talk to my older brother, Martin. He just got married and should be sort of an expert on sex.

I wait outside Martin and Karen's house for a few minutes because I don't want to interrupt something—with them being newlyweds and all—but it turns out they're on the patio, varnishing a china cabinet. I guess that's the sort of thing you do when you first get married.

Karen offers me some lemonade, and while she's

132

inside getting it, I come right out and say, "I need to know about sex."

Martin's a junior member of Dad's law firm and acts sort of like Dad. He puts down his brush and looks at me for a few seconds. I can hear Karen emptying ice-cube trays in the kitchen, which means she'll be out soon. "Quick!" I say.

"What is it you want to know?" he asks.

"Everything."

"Everything? Even the basics?"

"I *know* the basics. We learned all the technical stuff in sex ed. I want to know other stuff: like how you find a girl, and how you make sure she wants to, and—"

"This conversation is getting very sexist," says Martin, straightening his glasses. "The key word is respect!" He looks at me as if that explains the whole thing.

"Now you sound like Dad!"

He doesn't look displeased. "Well, why don't you talk to Dad about this?"

"What does Dad know about sex?"

My folks really drive me nuts lately. I remember Martin felt the same way about Ma and Dad when he was living at home, but I guess he doesn't remember.

Karen comes onto the porch with a pitcher of lemonade and three glasses. She's wearing a pair of shorts and a work shirt, and you know just by looking at her that any guy she's married to has got to be a sex expert. "So what's up, guys?" she asks.

Martin says, "Dave just wanted to ask me some questions about—"

"Fishing!" I shout. "I had questions about fishing. I'm going fishing tomorrow."

Karen says, "Martin doesn't fish."

"Neither does Davie," he says, and starts laughing. I can already hear him telling her the whole story as soon as I leave.

I drain my lemonade, then head for school, saying, "I leave you as a pedestrian, but will return as a driver!" I wonder how they'll spend the rest of the afternoon: varnishing the chest, talking about me, or making whoopee. "Making whoopee" is Grandma's term for sex. She also calls it "S-E-X."

The driver's-ed class is taught at my high school. Not *in* my high school exactly, but in a flimsy-looking shack about a half block away. Outside the shack, on the driving range, a rainbow-colored assortment of Buicks glimmers in the sunshine. I wonder if I'll get a chance to drive this afternoon.

Inside I only recognize two kids from my own high school. Although Martin would definitely find it sexist, I appraise the female portion of our class. Some of them are wearing short-shorts. It seems funny to see girls dressed like that in school, but I'm not complaining.

A hand touches my arm. A voice asks, "Are you

134

a student here? Do you know anything about this school?"

The girl sitting in front of me is twisted around in her seat, one hand on my arm, the other on my desk. She is wearing a green cotton shirt and shorts. The sun is shining through the window and lights up each strand of her long red hair. Her eyes are bright and green, open and trusting. She has freckles! Although I've lived in a state of perpetual passion since puberty, it's the first time I've ever felt as if all my circuits are overloaded. It is also the first time in my life I have been speechless.

She repeats her question, and somehow I find my voice. I'm working on a mellow baritone, but sometimes a bass or soprano comes out. Of course, this has to be one of the times I sound like Minnie Mouse. I say, "Yes, I go to school here. What do you need to know?"

"I'm a little nervous about this class. I've heard it's really hard," she says.

I snap my fingers. "It's a piece of cake, believe me! Like everything else at Nolan Keith High School, our driver's ed is hopelessly behind the times. I mean, every other school in the world has on-the-street driving as part of the class, but do we get to cruise the expressways of our fair city? I should say not! We drive around that dumb little track out behind this shack." I'm talking too fast, which I always do, and I'm talking too much, which I sometimes do.

"What about the teacher?" she asks.

"A real pushover." Actually I know the class is taught by this grizzled old ex-Marine who insists on being called *Sgt.* Bering and is known as the meanest S.O.B. east of the Mississippi, but I don't want to scare the girl.

The girl turns away, looking greatly relieved.

She begins to study a magazine and take notes, looking very studious. Within five seconds I'm homesick for the sight of her face, so I tap her on the back. "What are you reading?"

She turns the periodical so I can see the cover. It's *The American Journal of Clinical Pathology.*

"What are you, a doctor?" I say.

She doesn't laugh. Instead, she nods and says, "Not yet, but I plan to be!"

"Wow," I say, because I'm really impressed. But I'm also a little worried. Obviously she's a gifted overachiever. What will she think of a gifted under-achiever like me?

"Who's this month's centerfold?" I say, taking the mag from her hands. I flip through it and show her a picture of some hemoglobin. "Miss August. Doesn't she get your blood pumping?"

The girl looks at me like she's never heard anyone crack a joke before. As she reaches for the maga-zine, the door of the shack slams and we hear: "Ten-*shun*!"

Sgt. Bering must think he's teaching a bunch of pinheads, because the first thing he says is, "The

136

purpose of a driver's education class is to teach you how to drive." Then he pauses for almost fifteen seconds to let this profound information seep into our brains.

I look at the seat in front of me. My new best friend is writing this statement down in her notebook.

After telling us a few more things about driver's ed ("A car is an important but dangerous vehicle" and "Driving is a responsibility and a privilege"), he hands out our textbook, *Defensive Driving*, and a pamphlet called *What Every Driver Must Know*. He says we will sit in alphabetical order, and when he calls our names we should say our age and what school we come from and move to the appropriate seat. "Apple?" he barks.

This kid stands up. "I'm Lenny Apple, I'm sixteen, and I go to school here at Nolan Keith."

Bering points to the first seat, first row, for Lenny Apple.

It doesn't take all that long to get to the R's. I get up and say, "David Ross. David *W.* Ross. Sixteen. Nolan Keith High School."

Bering points to the seat right in front of me. The seat currently occupied by the budding doctor. It's okay because she has to get up to give her info next anyway. Her name is Sands.

When she gets up, I realize that Sands is a giant among women. Literally. I'm five foot six, but she towers over me. She's at least five eleven. Maybe six feet. Some of the kids are laughing at the two of us standing there next to each other. We must look like a Great Dane and a Yorkie. An ostrich and a hummingbird. The Jolly Green Giant and the Little Green Sprout.

She says, "I'm Molly Sands, and I'm sixteen."

Bering says, "Where do you come from, Sands?" The kids are still laughing, and I'm going nuts. I like *making* jokes. Not being one.

So I say, "From the Valley of the Jolly—ho, ho, ho—Green Giant."

Everyone laughs. Except the Jolly Green Giant.

Then I think: Jolly, Molly. Not bad.

When we're all in our final seats, I'm right in front of Molly Sands. Bering begins the first lesson, "What is defensive driving?"

Everyone begins making notes. I turn around and whisper, "Hey."

Without looking up, she says, "No."

"What do you mean, 'No'? I haven't even asked you the question yet."

"The answer would be no regardless of the question." She still hasn't looked up from the textbook.

"Why?"

"Because you're an obnoxious person."

"I was only going to ask to borrow a pencil."

"The answer is no."

"Why?"

"Because you're an obnoxious person."

I decide that now would not be a good time to

give Jolly Molly Sands The David W. Ross Simple Four-Question Sex Test.

That night Martin knocks on my bedroom door. "Hi, I just came over to drop off some briefs for Dad."

"What kind? Fruit of the Loom?"

"Someday that mouth of yours will earn you a fortune," he says, then throws a pamphlet on my bed.

"What's this?" I ask.

"You were asking about sex, right? Well I found this at the used bookstore. I haven't read it, but maybe it'll help."

"Forget about sex," I say—and it's the first time I've ever said *that*. "I've got bigger problems now. Marty, I've met this girl!"

"Oh, no," he says, "not another crush."

"It's not a crush!" A crush is something you get on your English teacher, or the lady who works the lunch counter at Woolworth's.

"Is it one-sided?" he asks.

"Well . . . so far."

"Then it's a crush."

"I only met her today, but there's this one little problem. . . ."

"What's the problem?"

"She thinks I'm obnoxious."

"You *are*!"

"Listen, just tell me how to get back into her good

139

graces and I'll be your slave for life! I'll wash your car every Saturday, mow your lawn every week. Anytime you want I'll come over to your house and scratch your back."

"I've got Karen to scratch my back," he says.

I wish I had someone like Karen. Someone to scratch *my* back. Someone like Molly.

"Marty, what am I going to do?"

"You could start by telling this girl you're sorry for whatever obnoxious thing you've done to her."

"Sorry?" I say. "That word's not in my Webster's." I don't know why it's so hard for me to apologize to people, but it just makes me feel very small to have to say that word. And feeling small was what got me into this.

"If you can't do a simple thing like apologize—" he begins, sounding exactly like Dad. So I tune him out and try to think of some way of establishing peace between Molly Sands and myself. I'd like to do something that would let her know I like her, something that would make her laugh, something that would be special between just the two of us.

After Martin leaves, I thumb through the pamphlet he brought me. It's called *You're Growing Up* and was published by Swiss monks in "The Year of Our Lord Nineteen Hundred and Sixty-one." I don't know how it can do me much good considering this is the Year of Their Lord about thirty years later, and besides, we're Jewish. I thumb through the pages, which have pictures of a nerd with tan pants and

140

black plastic glasses talking to a monk wearing a long robe with a rope around the middle. The main point of this sex booklet is: Don't do it. The whole thing is in the form of a conversation between the monk and the nerd.

Q. Is sex wrong?
A. Sex is not wrong within the context of a Catholic marriage.
Q. What do I do about "uncontrollable urges"?
A. Exercise, cold showers, and study will help to take your mind off these unfortunate, but very natural, urges. Prayer is also helpful for some boys.

The pictures in the booklet show the nerd and the monk walking down a country road, sitting on a stone wall, standing on a beach gazing at the water. In just about *every single* picture, the monk has his hand on the nerd's shoulder or back. I mean, are you thinking what I'm thinking? The last page of *You're Growing Up* is an application form for the monastery. Before throwing the booklet in the trash, I mail the application to Switzerland with Martin's name on it.

Just before going to bed, I get a great idea for a peace offering. I sneak down to the kitchen and grab a can of Jolly Green Giant Garden Fresh Peas. If that doesn't make her love me, I don't know what will.

It doesn't make her love me. In fact, she tosses the can of peas out the open window of the shack.

I try to hide my disappointment. "I thought you'd like it," I say. "It was a peas offering. Get it?"

Her expression doesn't change. She has the most amazing eyes—like gold nuggets lightly painted over with green. When she's mad, like now, the gold parts get even brighter. "Maybe it's just me," she says, sighing. "But I find your attempts at humor really immature."

"Oh, come on, Jolly—"

"And *why* do you keep calling me that name?"

I don't think it's the right time to tell her Jolly is my pet name for her. It's a lot better than "lovebug," "snugglesnooks," "my little marshmallow," or any of the fifteen million endearments I've heard other people use. Instead I tell her, "Oh, it's just a nickname. You know, I've always wanted one. Something with a little more zip than David Ross. I tried adding my middle initial, W, but even that doesn't really help."

"Well, *I* don't want one!" she says.

"But it suits you!" I say.

"I am not a jolly person!" she shouts, pounding on her desk.

"No, but that's part of the joke. Like calling a big fat guy 'Tiny.' "

She stares at me. "Would you call an overweight person 'Tiny'?"

"Sure, why not?"

"You are so insensitive," she says, opening her textbook.

"If you want me to quit calling you 'Jolly,' I will."

She looks up. "You really mean that?"

"I really mean it, Jolly." I swear on my life that I meant to say "Molly" just then, but the other word just slipped out. It's her eyes that did it! And what else can I do then but laugh? Her face turns red and her eyes squinch up, and even as I laugh, I know I'll never be able to call her by her correct name again.

For the rest of the afternoon she ignores me, and that night I call Martin. "She doesn't like my jokes!"

"Smart girl," he replies.

"That's another problem," I say. "She's supposed to be this big brain, but she thinks I'm borderline retarded."

"I thought you had the highest I.Q. at Nolan Keith."

"Let's put it this way: Last year I didn't crack a book outside the classroom and still got all A's. But she's one of those *show-offy* types. Carries around a ton of books. Reads medical journals. I'm more the laid-back type."

"You're more the undisciplined type."

"But the very worst thing," I say, "is that she's taller than me. A *lot* taller than me."

"How much?"

"Five inches."

"Don't worry about it," he says. "Lots of guys don't get their growth spurt till they're seventeen, eighteen years old."

"I've spurted!" I shout. "I've already spurted! I'm

not *going* to get any taller. Sgt. Bering says I'll have to sit on a telephone book to drive a car."

"Listen, I've got to get off here," he says.

"You've been a real help, big brother," I say, hanging up hard.

I hate when people brush me off like that. I hate being ignored. I don't want Molly Sands looking through me or past me or around me for the rest of the semester. I want her to look *at* me. I want her to talk to me. And I'll do anything to make sure she does.

So that's how it goes for the next three weeks. She tries to ignore me, and I do my best to get her attention. The day we all go outside to look under the hood of a car, I see the can of peas still lying on the ground. I shout, "Hey, look, everyone! That's where Jolly pea'd in the grass!" I'm rewarded with a lot of laughs from the kids and a glare from Molly.

A few days later Sgt. Bering displays traffic signs, and I explain to the kids in my row how the lines in the curves-ahead sign compare to Molly's anatomy. She kicks her foot against the desk when she hears that. I love to see her face when it turns the same color as her hair; it means she's listening. It means I'm getting to her.

Then it's time to actually learn how to drive. The four people in our row all get into the teacher's car, which is equipped with an extra set of brakes for Bering and a CB radio—which he can use for bitching at the other cars on the range. As we walk over to the car, Sandra Tremonti says, "I have to sit next to the window because I get carsick."

Bob Westberg is the first to drive, so he gets behind the wheel while Sandra, Molly, and I get into the backseat. I am seated between the two girls. "Oh, no!" says Molly. "I'm not sitting next to *him.*" She says the word "him" with the same inflection most of us reserve for the word "mucous."

"What's wrong, Jolly? Afraid you won't be able to keep your hands off me?"

She ignores that. "Sit in the middle, Sandra," she says.

"But—but I get carsick," Sandra says in her whiny voice.

"I'd rather have you vomit in my lap than sit next to him."

Bob Westberg drives perfectly around the outside track. Bering tells him it won't be long before he earns his own car to drive around the range. Bob looks pleased when he gets into the backseat with Molly and me. "Great!" she says, patting his hand.

Now *I* feel like vomiting. Especially when I view Bob objectively from head to toe and see no visible flaws except one small scab the size of a quarter on his knee.

In the front seat Sandra holds her arms out straight like a sleepwalker and squeezes the wheel like a sponge. She pulls onto the track and we begin our journey. Suddenly—*skree-ee*-uhk!—she slams on the brakes, and Bob, Molly, and I all fly forward. "What the hell are you doing?" shouts Bering.

"But there's a little bird up there on the track," she says. "I don't want to run him over."

Bering says, "I'll tell you what, Tremonti. Next time you see a bird on the track, I just want you to roll down your window very gently, stick your head outside, and say, 'Get off the track, little birdie. I don't want to hurt you.' Have you got that?"

"Yes, I think so."

She starts moving again, and we are halfway down the other side of the track when—*skree-ee*-uhk! I pull my face from the back of Sandra's seat just in time to see her roll down the window, stick her head outside, and say, "Get off the track, little birdie. I don't want to hurt you."

I'm laughing so hard I can't hear Sgt. Bering yell at her. Even Molly and Bob are trying not to laugh. Molly is rubbing her forehead from where she knocked against the back of Bering's seat. I say, "Gosh, Jolly, we've only been out in the car together once and already you're knocked up."

I can't see Molly's face, but Bob looks like he wants to punch me in the eye.

When it's my turn to drive, I follow our textbook instructions to a T. I walk 360 degrees around the car, checking to see if the tires are low, making sure there is no broken glass in the path of the car. Then get in, lock the door, and fasten my seat belt. Adjust the mirrors, start the car. It roars to life under my hands. "Ready?" says Bering.

"Ready," I say, shifting into drive.

The Buick moves.

I feel totally in control as I maneuver the car down the track. The window is down and a cool breeze whips my hair. We are approaching the first turn, and I flip on the indicator, then slowly round the bend.

Bering says, "You might want to speed it up a little."

I glance at the speedometer and see I'm driving only three MPH. Well, it seemed like a lot more than that. I press on the accelerator and watch the needle climb to six MPH. I wonder if Molly is impressed. As we travel down the longest side of the track at a steady clip, I wish I were wearing a pair of sunglasses. The sky is blue, the engine purrs, and the girl I love is sitting right behind me as the road rolls beneath my wheels.

The front of the car seems to lift into the air, as if the Buick is going to take off flying. I realize too late that it's doing that because I'm going up over the curb. I've missed my second turn completely and now the front wheels are rolling across the grass into the bushes. The only reason we don't hit the fence is because Bering slams on his brakes at the last moment.

For all the time I've spent trying to make Molly

laugh, this is the only time I've succeeded. Bob Westberg smiles out the window, and Sandra Tremonti tugs on Molly's sleeve, whispering, "This guy drives like a maniac!"

Bering says it will probably be some time before I earn my own car to drive on the track. When I get into the backseat, Bob's knee is pressed against Molly's knee—and she doesn't pull it away.

At the beginning of each class period, Sgt. Bering announces who has earned a car. Bob Westberg is the first person in the class to get his own car, and everybody—except me—gives him a big round of applause. Molly gets her car a couple days later, and I say out loud to the class, "Gee, I'm going to miss the fun we used to have in the backseat, Jolly."

She stands to get her car keys from Bering. "Do you know what sexual harassment is?" she says.

"Don't worry, Jolly. I *like* it when you harass me!"

"You're going to pay for it someday," she warns.

"You mean you're going to start charging me for it?" I say.

Some people laugh, a couple say "Woo!" and even I'm beginning to think I'm going too far with this stuff. But I'm afraid to stop. Because if I stop, she won't notice me *at all*.

Pretty soon almost everyone in the class has earned a car to drive around the track. It's fun to watch them putt-putt around the range, three car lengths apart, obeying various signs and the traffic signal at one of the cross sections. I'm watching them because I still haven't earned a car yet. In fact, only two students in the class are still driving with the teacher— Tremonti and me. I wonder what went wrong. Sgt. Bering says I'm too easily distracted. But I'm only distracted when Molly is driving nearby.

To illustrate: One day I'm driving with Bering, and we pass Molly coming up the road facing the outside lane. I honk the horn and wave. Bering slams on his side of the brakes. "Never, *never*, NEVER use the horn as anything other than a warning instrument," he shouts. Another time I'm driving with Bering and see Molly and Bob Westberg talking outside the shack. I run a stop sign.

It's not until two weeks before the end of the class that I finally get my own car. When Sgt. Bering informs me of this momentous occasion, everyone except Molly applauds. "You're the only person in the class who didn't give me the clap," I tell her as we walk outside to the cars.

"I'd like to give you a lot more than that," she snaps, striding away.

"Is that a promise?" I call after her.

It feels really strange to be sitting in a car without Bering beside me and Sandra in the backseat. As I insert the key into the ignition, I tell myself I want to remember this day forever. My first solo driving experience! Molly is coming down the home stretch as I start car number five. I flip on my turn signal and pull onto the road, cutting her off. She shakes her fist, and I throw back my head, laughing. She looks so pretty when she's angry.

I've got the turn signal on again, getting ready to make my first solo left turn. Slow down, don't brake, nice and smooth. Perfect! The speedometer quivers between nine and ten MPH as I round that curve. I'm surprised when I see Molly turn the corner right after me. It doesn't seem like she's the required three car lengths behind. If anything, she seems to be getting even closer. I'm watching the road ahead, but my eyes keep shifting to the rearview mirror. She's two car lengths behind, maybe only one. I speed up to widen the space, but it doesn't help. It almost looks as though she's speeding up too.

Bering's voice squawks over the CB: "Car number one, watch those car lengths. I repeat, car number one, watch those car lengths."

But she's not slowing up.

I step on the gas. I'm going fourteen MPH. That's faster than I've ever gone. She's still on my tail. I speed up, Bering tells me to slow down, I whip around the next corner without a turn signal. *She's right behind me.*

Car number nine is crawling along in front of me, and I've got to slow down before I rear end it. But Molly is no more than three yards behind my fender and getting closer. I speed up, looking back over my shoulder. Molly's face is red and her mouth is set. I can tell she's determined, despite the other cars, despite Bering's wrath, to run me off the road!

I lay on my horn, and car number nine, driven by Bob, pulls over to the side. Horn blowing may be an unpardonable sin in Bering's eyes, but I've got to get moving before she rams me.

Other cars are pulling to the side of the track. Even the teacher's car. Only Molly and I are left, but we're zipping around like we're on a racetrack. Twenty miles per hour. Twenty-five. She's determined to get me, all right.

Racing around and around the track, zipping through stop signs and red lights, passing the big gate leading out of the range, I feel like I'm inside Ma's blender. And Molly is only a few feet off my rear. I know that as long as we continue whipping around the little track, the chances are good she's going to rear end me. I fleetingly wonder if I shouldn't just pull over and stop the car, but I have the feeling she'll just go ahead and crash into me anyway.

No, I've got to get off this track, put some distance between us. And so the next time the gate leading out of the range nears, I whip through it and zoom out onto the street. Let's see her follow me now. But sure enough, she's got her turn signal on. Turn signal! Even when she's breaking all the rules, she's "driving defensively"! She zips out the gate and bears down on me. Bering is screaming every four-letter word ever invented over the CB, and I hear him yell at Sandra, "Follow those cars!"

"But—but Sgt. Bering, I don't think I'm ready for street driving yet."

"Get that goddamn foot on the gas pedal!" he bellows.

It's a little amazing to be driving in the street just like a real person. I'm going thirty MPH down Limepole Street, and Molly is right behind me. I'm trying to drive around the perimeters of Keith Playfield, where it's unlikely we'll meet up with any other drivers, but after a couple times around the field I realize the only improvement in our situation is that we've traded the little round school range for a slightly bigger range. Molly is still behind me, I'm still sweating gallons, and we're still playing dodge-'em cars.

Only we're not "playing" anything, and it's not funny. It's scary.

Way off behind Molly's car, I see Sandra and Bering coming down the street in the teacher's car. Sandra drives a few yards, slams on the brakes, drives a few yards, slams on the brakes.

It's not a question of what will happen if Molly hits me. Because I'm no longer thinking in terms of "if." I'm thinking "when." And I know that after she slams into me, Sandra will slam into Molly.

Responsible for a three car pileup! Before I even get my license!

I decide the only way to save the situation—or at least save the Buick—is to ditch it. If I can just get far enough ahead of Molly to pull over and abandon it, maybe I can run to someplace small—like a manhole—where her car won't fit.

I put every ounce of my weight on the gas pedal, speeding ahead to make a sharp right turn. I drive up over the curb—this time on purpose—and across the field. In the mirror I see two perfectly parallel plowed paths of playfield extending from my tires. I also see the Jolly Green Giant roaring up over the curb and hurtling toward me.

But I think I've got enough distance, so I pull the car toward the tennis courts. I *skree-ee-*uhk to a stop the way Sandra does and tear off my seat belt. Over the CB I hear Bering shout, "Drive over that curb, Tremonti!"

"But—but I'm *carsick*, Sgt. Bering."

I'm running toward the tennis court, thinking there's no way Molly's Buick could fit between the little gate leading to the courts. But then I see she's stopping her car beside mine, and in a second she's running toward me, fists clenched, face red, hair shining in the setting sun. She grabs a broken tennis racquet from the grass and catches me on the courts. The racquet comes down hard on my shoulders. "No more!" she shouts. "Look how crazy you've made me!"

God help me, but I can't stop with the mouth even now. "I knew I'd drive you crazy eventually," I say.

The hard wood bangs at my back and shoulders. The teacher's car pulls up, and since I don't hear *skree-ee-*uhk, I surmise Sandra has finally learned how to brake properly. I do hear the sound of Sandra barfing, however. Sgt. Bering yanks Molly off my

153

back, and I collapse to the ground. "I'm not through with him yet!" she shrieks as Bering pulls her away and I sit in the center of Keith Playfield at sunset, stunned into silence—beaten and crushed.

I've logged a lot of hours in the school office due to my "childish antics," as one of my teachers referred to them, but this is the first time I've looked out the window and seen the sun going down. Sandra is lying on one of the benches, a dripping paper towel plastered to her forehead. Molly and I sit on another bench, but as far apart as is humanly possible.

Our parents are inside talking to the summer-school principal.

I didn't know what to expect when Ma and Dad showed up, but they didn't yell at me in front of everyone else. . . . Of course, they don't know the whole story yet either. When they do, I may be grounded for the rest of my life.

I listen to the minutes click by on the office clock, and finally I say it: "Why did you do it?"

She turns to face me, and her mouth is drawn into a tight line. "What's the matter, baby? Haven't you ever had a girl chase you before?"

I can feel my mouth drop open in shock. Those were the last words I ever expected to hear from her. They sound ugly. Mean.

"We could have had an accident. We could have been killed!" I say.

"Hey, honey, when you're in love, that's just the chance you've got to take," she says, shrugging.

"Cut it out," I say. "I'm serious."

"It's not much fun when the shoe's on the other foot, is it?"

"What do you mean? I was just goofing around before. It wasn't anything serious. *This was serious!* We could have gotten hurt."

"I *have* been hurt. All summer long."

For the first time in my life, I can't find the right words to say. She keeps staring at me with those green-gold eyes, and finally I hear my voice saying, "I'm sorry."

"I find that hard to believe."

"You'd believe it if you knew how hard it is for me to say that. I'm sorry. I know you must think I've been a real S.O.B. this summer . . . but I have good reasons."

"Oh, sure!" Sandra moans from her bench.

And then I tell Molly something that's even harder to say than "I'm sorry." I tell her, "See, I like you."

"You never stop, do you? Quit playing those stupid games!"

But how can I tell her I finally have stopped? I say: "From that first day in class, there was just something about you that I really liked. I don't know for sure what it was. Is. But I couldn't stop looking at you, or thinking about you. I guess we're completely different types, but I felt like you knew things I didn't know. You sat there reading that medical magazine,

155

and I thought that if I wasn't me—the person I am—I'd be like you."

"Ha!" she says.

"I've got a serious side too, you know. It's buried pretty deep, but you made me think about it. And I thought you might even have a funny side. . . . I mean, I wanted to ask you out right then and there!"

"Why didn't you?"

My heart pauses mid-beat. "Would you have gone out with me?"

"No."

"See? I couldn't stand that, if you said no. And I couldn't stand it that you tried to ignore me. I had to do something to make you think about me."

She laughs bitterly. "Oh, I thought about you all right."

I remember Martin saying, "The key word is respect!" and I wish I'd listened a little more back then. I tell Molly, "I wish we could just rewind these last few weeks. So we could do it all over again. I wish I had another chance."

She looks me in the eye for a minute. "Do you know what it's like for a guy to harass you like that? Constantly? In front of the whole class?" I shake my head no. She says: "It hurts."

"I guess it does. . . . Probably not as much as getting hit by that tennis racquet. . . ." But I look at her face and I'm not so sure. It's the second time she's told me how much it hurts. And now that I really look into her eyes, I see how they've changed. They don't look open and trusting anymore. They look scared. Angry. I can only say it again. "I'm sorry. I'm really sorry for everything . . . Molly."

She gets up and walks from the office. "Tell my parents I'm waiting in the hall."

When she leaves, I whisper, "Oh, God, I really screwed that one up, didn't I?"

"You sure did!" says Sandra Tremonti.

"I was a jerk."

"You sure were!" says Sandra.

The door opens and Molly returns. She looks around blankly; then her eyes rest on me as if it's the first time she's ever seen me. "Excuse me," she says politely. "I'm looking for my parents."

"Huh?" I say.

"My parents told me to meet them here," she says, walking toward me and smiling hesitantly.

"Are you okay?" I ask. "You didn't have a concussion or something when we were fighting, did you?"

"I don't believe we've met," she says, extending her hand. "I'm Molly Sands."

"I don't get it," I say.

From her bench Sandra Tremonti moans, "Geez-o-Pete, I get it and I've got my eyes shut. I get it and I'm in the middle of a nervous breakdown. I get it and—"

Finally, I get it too.

"Hi, Molly," I say, taking her hand. "I'm David

Ross. David W. Ross. And it's a pleasure to meet you."

We didn't get arrested or sent to prison for the big car chase. We did flunk driver's ed, though. Now it's September, and both Molly and I are taking the after-school driving class with Sgt. Bering. Usually after class we hang around and talk.

Yesterday we kissed for the first time.

Molly and I never talk about the things that happened to us before we met that evening in the principal's office. This past summer seems like it happened to someone else—some jerk I used to know a long time ago.

Although I may not run around giving girls The David W. Ross Simple Four-Question Sex Test anymore, don't think I've stopped thinking about sex. I haven't changed *that* much!

When it comes right down to it, I guess I have to hand it to those monks. They really knew what they were talking about. To illustrate: I've come to the conclusion that cold showers *do* help—except when you imagine another person in the cold shower with you.

And they were right about something else: Prayer helps. Sometimes when I'm lying in bed at night, thinking about how good it feels to know someone like Molly and how close I came to screwing it up, I whisper into the darkness, "Please, God, please. Don't ever let me be such a jerk again."

Mad

Sometimes when no one was looking, I would sneak into the chapel. Not for a moment's peace, but for a moment—madness.

Except for Sunday mornings, the Grey Oaks chapel was strictly off-limits to students. Yet whenever there was a rainstorm, I'd go there and listen to the wind howl. There was a large window behind the altar, and the storm would slap big red and yellow leaves to the glass. I liked to look past the leaves at the huge black clouds. Later, the sun would shine through the leaves, and I'd remember the stained-glass window at my previous boarding school. This window, with the red and the yellow, the sunlight and blue sky, was even more impressive.

I had been to many boarding schools. But this one was different.

Grey Oaks was the first school I'd been to where

159

I felt like one of the guys. I was making friends. I was following the rules. So even I was a little surprised that stormy day in October when Paige Browne asked, "Want to head over to Maddy's for a burger?" and I shook my head no. That wasn't like me. And it wasn't like me when, later, in the hallway, Drake Longhorn and P. J. Gimble asked if I wanted to go to the arcade and I said no again.

A few minutes later I found myself inside the chapel, letting my eyes adjust to the darkness. The heavy oak door shut with a slow, sucking sound, as if I were being sealed into a tomb. Outside the window, the sky had turned the color of an angry bruise, and a fierce wind whipped the maple branches. Something seemed to untwist inside my chest. I took a deep breath, and then I heard it.

Someone began to play the organ.

It was sad music. It was also very loud. I knew it wasn't old Mrs. Snites, the woman who played the organ during services every Sunday morning. She couldn't play very well. *But this organist!* . . . Before I realized it, I was moving up the twisting stairway to the loft, as if the music were pulling me.

I stood on the top step and stared. A girl was sitting at the organ. I could only see her from the back, but she looked about eleven. She was wearing a white corduroy jumper over a white blouse. The little gooseneck lamp hanging from the top of the organ lit up pale hair as short and fine as a baby's. Her head did not move as her hands boomed up and down the keyboard. It sounded as if she were playing with thunder. I could feel the music in my fingers and toes and teeth. When she finished the song, I turned to go downstairs. The plate-glass window continued to rattle, distorting my favorite view of the wet red and yellow leaves.

"I know someone's there," she said, without turning around. "Don't try sneaking out."

"It's just me," I said, then wanted to pound myself into the ground like a stake. What a stupid thing to say! I hadn't spent a lot of time around girls, and I always seemed to screw up when I tried to talk to them. I amended my statement: "I'm Henry Tremain."

"Oh," she said, still not turning.

I was surprised by the response. Usually people said, "Henry Tremain!" and I'd quickly add, "Junior!" Or they'd look at me carefully and say, "You aren't any relation to *the* Henry Tremain are you?" and I'd have to admit that yes, I was his son.

My dad was one of the nation's top business executives. I always said I hated not having my own identity, but when people *didn't* react to the name, I couldn't help but feel a little lost.

The girl said, "I guess you want to know my name now," and she leaned over the keyboard so that her forehead rested on the music holder. Then she picked out a simple tune with the fingers on her right hand. After a moment, she said, "That is my name."

"I don't get it." The music was a little familiar,

happy like a Scottish jig, but I didn't know what it had to do with anything.

She sighed. " 'Jesu, Joy of Man's Desiring.' Commonly known as 'Joy.' . . . That is my name." She turned around, and I realized she wasn't ten or eleven years old, as I'd thought. She looked closer to my age, fifteen. Her face was calm, but her eyes were a piercing blue. She stared at me, then said loudly, "Joy Glass."

"Oh, no," I said, as soon as I heard the infamous last name. "Don't tell me you're Young Mr. Glass's daughter? Old Mr. Glass's granddaughter?"

She nodded twice.

Mr. Glass, the headmaster, was about forty-five years old and looked like a character from *Goodbye, Mr. Chips.* It must have been his spectacles. Most people have frames that hook over their ears; his didn't even have frames—they pinched onto his nose. He had inherited the school from his father, Old Mr. Glass, an antique man who followed his son around as if he were attached with an invisible leash.

Joy Glass looked at me defiantly. "Don't worry," she said. "I hate them too."

"I don't hate them!" I said. "Your dad seems like a nice man, and I feel bad for your grandfather." Poor Old Mr. Glass was almost blind and couldn't say a word because of a long-ago stroke.

"Oh, for pity's sake!" Joy said in disgust. "Don't tell me you believe all those lies."

"What lies?"

162

She rolled her eyes up to the eaves of the chapel. "Oh, that he can't talk."

"But he can't!"

"Yes, he can! You should hear him at home. He never shuts up!"

"Why would anyone lie about *that*?" I asked, perplexed.

"Oh, they lie about *everything!* What religion do you think we are?"

"Episcopalian, I guess." After all, Grey Oaks was an Episcopal school.

"Jewish!" said Joy. "We're Jewish, but we have to pretend we *aren't* because it's an Episcopal school."

I couldn't think of anything worse than having to pretend you were something you weren't. I felt sorry for her.

But I had another thought as well. I had been at Grey Oaks for several weeks and had never seen a girl around; I'd never heard that Mr. Glass and his wife had any children. The Glasses and Old Mr. Glass lived in a building on campus known as the Glass House. "Do you live here?" I asked.

"Live?" she sighed. "No, I don't *live* here. I exist here." I thought that was a little dramatic, but when tears began to glisten in the light from the gooseneck lamp, I reconsidered. She got up from the bench and moved to the loft railing, staring at the rain beyond the window. "Until yesterday I lived, very happily I might add, in Boston, at the Flanders School. Now they've brought me back here to be with them."

163

"Why?" I asked.

Tears were streaming down her face, but she didn't make a sound. It was eerie. Finally she said, "Do you know what it's like to be someplace you don't want to be? Do you know what it's like to leave everyone and everything you love?"

My chest was beginning to feel tight. For years I'd been in boarding schools I didn't want to be at, away from my dad and our housekeeper. I knew how she felt. But now, at Grey Oaks, I didn't feel that way. And I didn't *want* to remember feeling that way. I moved toward the stairs. "Look, I think I've got to be going," I said.

Then I felt her hand on my arm. Not just *on* my arm, but wrapped around it. Tightly, as if she were taking my blood pressure with her palm. "Help me," she whispered.

The fear in her voice, the pressure on my arm scared me, and I felt like I had to whisper too. "Help you what?"

Her voice got louder, her chin lifted defiantly, as if she were issuing a dare. "Help me escape."

Although I was still feeling aftershocks from my meeting with Joy Glass, it was good to be back in the familiar brown-and-gray dorm room. It was good to see Stephen Hall, my roommate, doing his usual thing: taking his pulse. The first time I saw Stephen—in late August when I arrived at Grey Oaks—he was seated on his bed, wearing jockey shorts, with his left foot pulled way up in front of his face. One hand held the foot, the other held *Taber's Medical Dictionary.* "Hi," he said, "I'm your roommate, but probably not for long. I think I've got a malignant melanoma between my toes."

Stephen was always dying of something.

I guess it would be a little easier to understand if he were a chalk-faced ninety-three-pounder with a heart murmur and leg braces, but that wasn't the case. Stephen was a big, husky guy with bright red cheeks who'd probably be better suited for the Mighty Oaks—our football team—than a hospital ward. And the fact that he was in love with Katie, the school nurse, probably didn't do much to cure his hypochondria.

Still, he was a nice guy, and we had no problems rooming together. And he was very understanding about my nightmares. Soon after I enrolled in Grey Oaks, I began to have horrible dreams filled with faceless beings screaming. I'd wake up yelling, but Stephen would always bring me a Dixie cup filled with water and lend me a George Winston cassette. Sometimes he'd tell me about his experiences with girls, and though I guessed most of them were fiction, I never said anything. And Stephen never said anything about my nightmares to any of the guys.

"Did you know Mr. Glass has a daughter?" I said.

He looked up from his pulse taking. "Not unless they grew her in a test tube," he said. "I've got it on good authority that Mr. and Mrs. Glass sleep in separate beds. Stewie Malks had to help roll the carpets in the Glass House last year, and he saw the beds."

"Well, I saw the daughter," I said importantly, strolling over to the dartboard, where Stephen joined me. Darts were our favorite pastime.

"What's she look like?" he asked. "On a scale of one to ten."

I always hated when someone asked me to rate a girl. Being around girls as seldom as I was, I thought they all looked like twelves.

"Oh, I don't know," I said, tossing a dart. "You'll have to judge for yourself."

"Why? How long's she going to be here?"

"Permanently, I think. She says she's going to school here."

That rattled Stephen so much, he missed the dartboard altogether. "A girl going to Grey Oaks? It isn't allowed!"

"Well, when your father's the headmaster . . ."

"Speaking of fathers," he said, nodding toward my desk, "you got a letter from yours."

"Why's he sending me a letter when I'll see him day after tomorrow?" Sunday was Parents' Day, and Dad was actually coming. I tore open the envelope and blocked out Stephen's comments about an honest-to-God *girl* at Grey Oaks while I read:

Dear Henry:
 I hope things are going well for you. Your letters

certainly sound like you're enjoying your new school. As you know, I was very much hoping to see it myself on Parents' Day, but I'm going to have to take a raincheck on it. This weekend I'll be in Aspen, of all places. Leave it to Raymond Motors to combine a ski weekend with a merger meeting. I know you'll understand, and I know

I stopped reading. No matter how many good letters I sent my dad, it seemed like I always got the same one in return. I should have known *something* would come up before Parents' Day.

"Bad news?" said Stephen as I came back to the dart game.

"Just the usual stuff," I said, sending a dart whizzing past his head.

"Careful!" he shouted. "I don't want my ear pierced."

I realized I was already feeling better. So Dad wasn't coming. That didn't make Grey Oaks any less great. It didn't take away my new friends, my new home. I looked out the window at the wet trees in the early darkness, then went back to playing darts.

I didn't see Joy Glass again for three days. On Saturday a bunch of us went horseback riding down Willowby Road. Mr. Glass and his wife drove past in their Cadillac, but Joy was not with them. Nor was she around on Parents' Day—not that I had a lot of time to look for her. The few of us without guests were drafted for punch-bowl and clean-up duty. I didn't mind, but P. J. Gimble, who stood pouring punch next to me, kept muttering, "Yeah, my parents need me to get straight A's, they need me to get into Harvard. But when *I* need *them*? . . . Orphaned!"

By Monday morning I was beginning to wonder if I'd imagined Joy Glass. "Maybe it's like a *Twilight Zone* episode," I told Stephen as he brushed his teeth. "You know, eventually I tell someone about her, and they look at me strangely and say, 'Joy Glass? Yes, the headmaster used to have a daughter named Joy, quite an organ player as I remember, but she was killed a long time ago in an avalanche.' "

Stephen laughed, then said, "Organ player? What do you mean by that?"

"Nothing. I'm just being weird," I said, then started humming the *Twilight Zone* theme music. I'd forgotten he didn't know where Joy and I met.

But when I got to my first class, Spanish, I found out she was not a product of my imagination. She was seated in the last seat of the first row. I waved when I saw her, but she stared ahead with eyes as blank as blue marbles. The teacher didn't introduce or even acknowledge her. That's how it went all day. None of the teachers acted as if it were at all strange to have a new student in the class. Even a girl student in an all-boys school. None of the guys knew how to react to her. Some of them tried to make small talk, but she definitely was not interested. Rumors started circulating that Mr. Glass would expel any student seen talking to his daughter.

And that's how it went for the next two weeks. Joy was there among us, but not really *with* us. She never raised her hand in class, but she always knew the answer when the teacher said, "Miss Glass?" In the dining room she sat by herself at a small table facing the window.

One day at lunch, P. J. looked over at Joy. "I always said I'd give anything to have a *girl* around here, but 'Miss Glass' is about the most stuck-up girl I've ever met in my life!"

"Stuck-up?" I said. For two weeks Joy Glass had looked right through me, yet I never thought she was stuck-up. I just thought she was feeling out of place. *I'd* certainly felt that way in the past, so I decided right then that it was my duty to break the ice. I got up from the table and walked toward Joy, disregarding P. J. and Stephen's startled comments. "Hi," I said. "You *do* remember me, don't you? Why don't we go over to Maddy's this afternoon and—"

She slowly lifted her head and stared at me. I remembered how hard she'd grabbed onto my arm in the chapel, and although this time her hands stayed in her lap, I felt she was pushing me away with her *eyes* now. "Go," she said. "Go away quick."

I had to slink back to my table, her words still ringing in my ears. I could barely hear the ribbing I was getting from the guys. . . . But when I got back

169

to my room that evening, there was a long white envelope under the door, half in the room, half out. I got a paper cut slicing the envelope with my index finger but forgot the sting as I pulled out a sheet of paper and read the two lines:

Meet me in the Woods tomorrow morning. I need help.

Every student at Grey Oaks knew about the Woods. That's what we called the wild area about half a mile behind campus. Like the chapel, it was off-limits to students—and that's the reason I kept looking over my shoulder as I hiked out there on Saturday morning. It was a blustery day, and my Grey Oaks standard-issue sweatshirt was not keeping me warm. I wondered how long I'd have to wait in the woods until she showed. *If* she did.

But she was already there. I found her sitting on the edge of a small cliff, eating from a large bag of nacho chips. She didn't offer me any, nor did she say hi. The first thing she said was: "Have you ever been in love, Henry Tremain?"

I had been stamping my feet up and down to get warm, but her question stopped me cold. "Well . . ." I began.

"I'm in love," she said, biting a nacho neatly in half. "I'm in love and I want to get married."

"To who?" I said.

"His name is Gil," she said. "Gil Gabhart. And I *am* going to marry him."

"You're not old enough to get married," I pointed out.

"Yes I am. In some states I am."

"What about *this* state?" I asked.

She jumped up and ran to a small tree near the edge of the cliff. The tree was curving in the wind, but she leaned around it, pushing it even closer to the ground. Bright yellow leaves shimmered around her head; the rushing air inflated her windbreaker like a balloon. And she began to scream.

I didn't know what to do. Was it some kind of a joke? Was she having a nervous breakdown? And why was she suddenly waving at me to come over and join her? She stopped screaming and said, "Try it."

"Try what?"

"Screaming into the wind. The wind absorbs the sound, thereby absorbing anger, unhappiness, and unresolved passions." She smiled at me. "Go ahead. Scream."

"Frankly, Joy, I don't have any anger, unhappiness, or unresolved passions."

"Everyone has them. Whether they know it or not." I didn't know how to tell her my life was pretty okay lately. It almost seemed rude to say it, considering the problems she seemed to be having. Her blue eyes flared, and she pointed a finger at me, commanding: "Scream, Henry Tremain!"

So I screamed.

I felt kind of silly, screaming into the wind. I didn't

feel anger and unhappiness leaving my body. Mostly I felt my throat getting sore.

Joy patted my arm and said, "You're almost there." She sat down, took a deep breath, and began eating nachos again. "When I was at the Flanders School, I found it necessary to scream at least fifteen minutes a day . . . and that was a good school. Here at Grey Oaks I think I should probably scream fifteen *hours* a day."

"Grey Oaks is a good school."

"Oh, for pity's sake!" she said, punching the ground with her fist. "Haven't you ever noticed that everyone here is . . . well, odd?"

"Thanks a lot!" I said.

"Think about it. You can start at the top—right at the top with my father—and go all the way down to the lowliest freshman."

"What's wrong with your father?"

"Does he seem like a real person to you? I mean, I live with the man and I swear to God sometimes I think he's a robot."

"I don't know. He helped me out when I had that trouble with my textbook." I told Joy about the history textbook I received my first week at Grey Oaks. The first day of class I opened it up and found that, despite the *American History 3* cover, there was a biology book sewn into the binding. Mr. Glass had personally contacted the text distributor and ordered a new one. When I finished telling her the story, Joy looked unimpressed.

172

"Big whoop," she said. "Textbooks! Why doesn't he tackle *issues*!" She got up and paced in the wind.

"What kind of issues?"

"Drugs! Sex! Racism! Violence! Peace! Or something as simple as why it's so damn impossible to be happy in this world."

"Most people are happy," I said.

"Not here they aren't. I don't know one genuinely happy, peaceful person in this whole school."

I was about to admit I was happy, but I could tell her mouth was poised for another "for pity's sake" if I attempted to contradict her.

She said: "Who's happy? My mother—who drives down to New York every other weekend to see another man? That creepy friend of yours who's always checking his pulse? You? Face it, how can *any* of the students be happy when they're obviously here because their parents don't want them at home?"

Something was banging on my ribs from the inside.

Then her whole demeanor changed. Her face seemed to get softer, her voice quieter. "Don't you think everyone should have their chance for happiness, Henry?"

"Well, yeah, of course."

"Don't you think *I* deserve it?"

"Yeah."

"Won't you help me then?"

"What do you want from me?"

173

"You know that little tape recorder you bring to class sometimes?"

I held my breath for a second. Sure, I brought it to class and taped lectures sometimes—but mostly I listened to Stephen's cassettes on it, nights I had my dreams. "What about it?" I asked.

"Can I borrow it?"

"That all you want? Just my tape recorder?"

"Just your tape recorder. And three hundred dollars."

The next morning, in church, I watched Joy from across the aisle. She was seated between her parents. Mrs. Glass was very pretty—if you liked older women. Every year Grey Oaks held a winter carnival, and Stephen told me last year's carnival featured a giant ice sculpture of Mrs. Glass. "And wasn't ice the perfect thing to make it from," he'd said.

Ever since that hour in the woods with Joy, I was seeing Grey Oaks in a different light. I didn't want to; yet every thought I had twisted itself into something negative. I hated that. I still wasn't sure why I agreed to her plan—because I truly wanted to help her, or just so that she would go away from Grey Oaks, taking my new attitude with her.

But I didn't want to get in trouble for helping Joy escape.

"It will be easy," she'd said, leaning forward and smiling. "I need the tape recorder so I can get a good head start, and I need the money to get to Boston."

"It doesn't cost three hundred dollars to get to Boston," I reminded her.

"Oh, I know, but food . . . and shelter. For pity's sake, it's not like you can't afford it!"

A few drops of rain were beginning to hit the treetops in the woods. It sounded like we were in a rain forest. I wondered if the only reason Joy was asking for my help was because In my pocket I always had cash, a Visa card, and a checkbook. But then . . . a lot of guys at Grey Oaks were loaded. I wasn't the only one. There must be something more she sees in me, I said to myself.

"How are you going to use the tape recorder?" I asked.

"Simple. Next week I'm going to ask my father if I can play the organ for church services."

"What about Mrs. Snites? She always plays it."

"Well, next week she won't. *I* will. Then I'll record the last song in advance, play the tape at the given time, and get the hell out of this place while everyone thinks I'm playing music like a good little girl."

"Isn't that kind of dramatic?" I asked. "Why don't you just leave whenever you want?"

She sighed. "Because on Sunday mornings the security guard comes in to the service." She spoke as if she were addressing a kindergartner.

I said, "Security isn't here to keep us from leaving. They're here to keep other people from coming onto the campus."

She raised her eyebrows and laughed. "Oh, is that what they tell you?"

It made me mad when she did that. And I still thought she was going to too much trouble to get out. I knew I could think of an easier way to get out—if I wanted to leave. I said, "How can you be sure your father will let you play the organ next week?"

"Easy. I'll just call him 'Daddy' a lot. Besides, he likes me to have interests."

The rain was coming down harder, and Joy put her head inside her windbreaker. The black, shiny material framed her face, made her look like a nun. Her voice grew quiet. "Oh, Henry, if you only knew what it's like to love something."

"I know what it's like to love something," I said, though not too convincingly.

"Oh, I don't mean something like hero sandwiches or jazz music. I don't even mean a person. I mean, yes, you love the person—but the *something* you love is that *thing* that you and that person have between you."

"You mean you're in love with love," I said.

The peaceful nun's face with the shiny white hair twisted in disgust. "Don't be a fool, Henry Tremain! I'm not asking you to understand. I'm just asking you to help me."

Again her hand was around my wrist, and this time I could feel her pulse pounding like a snare drum.

176

"I'll help you," I said, though I wasn't sure why.

As the service ended the next morning, I wondered if Joy had asked her father about playing the organ yet and how old Mrs. Snites would take the news. I wondered when I'd have to give Joy the money. And I wondered if she'd be happy once she got to Boston.

P. J. invited me for lunch at Maddy's, but I said no. Joy would be eating in the school dining room with her parents, and it was customary for Mrs. Snites to join the Glass family.

I sat as close as I could without being obvious, and although I was eating with Stephen, I spent most of my time peering over at the headmaster's table. Mr. Glass seemed to be discoursing on a long and boring topic. Mrs. Glass looked remote and untouchable; it was hard to believe she was having an affair with a man in New York. We'd always heard that her biweekly visits to the city were for the opera. I didn't think Mr. Glass had told Mrs. Snites yet, because she looked the same as always: Her face had the appearance of a melted candle, with drooping pale eyes and a long, thin nose. The corners of her lips quivered in the vicinity of her chin. Mrs. Snites was seated next to Old Mr. Glass, whose hand shook so much that by the time his soup spoon reached his mouth it was almost always empty. What odd people they are, I thought. And then I looked around the entire dining room and thought, what odd people we all are. George Adams, the president of the student body, sat next to his best buddy, Drew Hershey, looking like he wanted to kiss him. Little Elliot Northridge was stuffing hard rolls into his mouth as if he were a famine victim. Across the table, Stephen—who was practically glowing with good health—complained about kidney stones. And me . . . ? I wasn't sure what was wrong with me, but I felt like that history book I'd received: My outsides and insides didn't match.

And then I wondered how many people in the room were happy. And what right did Mr. and Mrs. Glass have to keep Joy from her chance for happiness?

I knew exactly when Mr. Glass broke the news to Mrs. Snites, because as soon as he told her she began choking on her cube steak. He patted her on the back, and Mrs. Glass tried to make her drink ice water. Old Mr. Glass just stared feebly on as Mrs. Snites gasped and kept saying, "I'm all right, don't touch me, I'm all right, don't touch me."

And while all this was happening, Joy slowly turned to me and smiled, mouthing out the word, "Victory!"

Two days later, I climbed the twisting stairway to the chapel loft again. I placed my tape recorder on top of the organ, along with an envelope containing six fifty-dollar bills.

When my alarm went off the following Sunday, I was already awake, staring out the window. Against a gray sky the trees were swaying back and forth as if a storm was brewing. I felt a storm brewing inside me too. I wanted to kick my feet against the bottom of Stephen's bunk and shout "Today's the day!" but of course I couldn't.

Instead I knocked against the bedpost and said, "Hey, Stephen. It's Sunday!" Only *I* knew the significance of those words.

"Wake me when it's Monday," he murmured, rolling over.

"Come on. You don't want to be late for services."

He moaned and slid off the bunk, heading for the bathroom. "There's got to be a better way to live," he muttered, slamming the door. Every morning there was that moan, and every morning brought some new ache, lump, or malignancy discovered just behind that door.

"Alopecia!" shouted Stephen, running from the bathroom half dressed.

"What's that?" I said, irritably.

"Baldness! I'm going bald!" He pulled back his thick dark hair to show me.

"Stephen," I said, "your hairline runs halfway down your forehead!"

"You can't see I'm going bald?" he shouted.

"Come on. Put *Taber's* away and let's get going to church."

He looked up from the dictionary, his eyes wide and sweat beginning to dot his forehead. "Henry, this is serious. Every hair on my entire body might fall out!"

Sometimes I thought every brain cell in his head had fallen out. It took fifteen minutes of reassuring to get him to church, but we still got there with time to spare.

I moved toward the front of the chapel and thumbed through a hymnal. Although nobody was seated in the first pews yet, I wanted my glance up to the loft to be as nonchalant as possible. When I did look, Joy popped over the railing in Snites's bulky black robe. No one was looking, so she flapped her arms like a huge bat getting ready to swoop down at me. It was good to see her happy for once. When I looked up a minute later, she was no longer visible. I knew I'd probably never see her again.

Usually, most of the guys were drowsy in chapel, but I think almost everyone noticed the difference in the music that Sunday. Heads turned, people whispered. I smiled down into the hymnal.

Normally on those Sundays that I couldn't work up an interest in the sermon, I would look through the clear glass window and, in my head, compose letters I knew I'd never write to my father. But that morning it was harder than ever to concentrate on the minister's words.

I held my breath when it was time for the last song. I thought the *click* of the tape recorder would sound like an explosion, but when the moment came, I didn't even hear it. The music sounded good. In fact, it sounded better than anything I'd ever heard Joy play. I could picture her running across the fields toward the road as we all sang with the music of my tape recorder.

When it was all over, I took my time leaving—first pretending I'd dropped something beneath the pew, then stopping to tie my shoe. When everyone was gone, including the minister, I climbed the twisting stairway that led to the loft. The black choir robe was thrown across the organ. And my tape recorder sat on top of the bench, humming as the rest of the blank tape played itself out.

That night, just after supper, all hell broke loose.

Stephen was studying biology; we were in the chapter on germs, so of course he was interested. I was sitting on the window seat watching the sky go from purple to black. Sometimes lightning would slice the sky; it was just beginning to rain. I wondered how many miles Joy had traveled. I thought the pounding on the door was thunder until George Adams stuck his head in and said, "Meeting of the minds! In the dining room! Now!"

Mr. Glass stood at the window in the dining room. At night the drapes were always closed, but he was pulling one back and staring through the rain-spattered windows. He looked stricken.

Then Mrs. Glass entered the room, still coolly

beautiful. But when she reached her husband, tears began to stream down her face. Stephen leaned over and whispered, "That's how the ice sculpture looked when it melted."

I laughed, but those tears definitely made me uneasy.

"I bet Old Mr. Glass died," Stephen whispered.

"I don't think so," I said.

All the guys in the dining room looked really concerned, and Mr. Glass didn't have to quiet the room before he began speaking. The first thing he said was "My daughter, Martha, is missing."

Martha? Her name was Joy. Although come to think of it, in class I'd never heard the teachers call her anything besides Miss Glass.

"We don't know exactly how long she has been missing," he continued, "but no one has seen her since chapel this morning."

Paige Browne, always a go-getter, jumped up and said, "Do you want us to search the grounds, sir?"

"That won't be necessary," said Mr. Glass. "Security has already conducted a very thorough search, and the police have been notified. However, I'm asking that if anyone has any type of information in regard to Martha's disappearance—or if anyone should see her, or find some clue as to where she may be, please let us know. Immediately."

Mrs. Glass stepped forward, but all she said was "Please."

Mr. Glass said, "Martha is a very sick girl. She needs medical attention. Every hour she's missing— every minute—" He stopped and turned to the window again.

After the meeting Mr. and Mrs. Glass retired to the Glass House. Some of the guys played Sherlock Holmes, walking outside with umbrellas to see if they could find some clues regarding Joy's disappearance. Stephen said, "I wonder if she ran away."

We were back in our room, getting ready for bed.

"What makes you say that?" I said, turning away to look out the window.

"I don't know," said Stephen. "And what do you think is wrong with her anyway?" He settled back into his pillows. "I mean, what if she's *really* sick? I once read about this diabetic Boy Scout who got lost on a camping trip without his insulin—and he went into a coma for three weeks. And there was this lady who always had fainting spells. One day she fainted on the sidewalk and drowned in a puddle of water only half an inch deep."

"Don't," I said, but in my mind I was replaying my conversations with Joy, trying to see if he could be right. No, I remembered her eating marshmallow cake in the dining room. She couldn't be a diabetic then, could she? And I'd never seen her faint. But still: "Martha is a very sick girl."

I thought, He's lying. He's lying, just like she said.

He just wants to keep her away from Gil. And her name isn't Martha. It's Joy. *She told me her name was Joy.*

It was the second night in a row I didn't sleep, and the next morning my nerves were pulled tighter than a high wire. All night long I'd thought of the various illnesses that Joy might have—and all the dangers of those illnesses. I was going to tell Mr. Glass where Joy was headed. After I told him, he and Joy—Martha—would have to work things out on their own. Maybe when he realized how desperate she was to be with the guy she loved—how far she was willing to go—he'd let her stay in Boston.

I knocked on his office door at eight thirty A.M. One look at his face and I knew I wasn't the only one who hadn't slept. In the corner sat Old Mr. Glass, staring out the window with his grainy white eyes.

"She's in Boston," I said, then turned to go.

As if it were that easy.

As if I didn't expect his hand to come down hard on my shoulder, turning my whole body around until I was face to face with the little glasses clipped to his nose, could see the red-and-pink veins running through the whites of his eyes.

"What did you say?"

"Your daughter is in Boston." That sounded almost rude to me, so I added: "I hope she's okay."

"What do you know about this?" he asked, panic and relief mingling on his face.

"She told me she was going to Boston—back to that Flanders School."

He took a deep breath, then picked up the telephone. I couldn't make out what he was saying, but I had the feeling Joy would be found within an hour.

When he hung up, he walked toward me. "Did she tell you *why* she was going back to Flanders?"

"To be with her boyfriend, Gil Gabhart."

"Oh, for pity's sake!" he said in disgust, turning away.

For one instant, he reminded me of my father. He didn't look like my father. It was just that motion— that turning away—that made them so alike.

I guess that's why I said what I did: I wanted to make him mad. "You can't face the truth, can you? Joy's right! You don't care about her! You're just a big liar!"

I'd never talked that way to an adult before. I didn't know what he would do to me. "Is that what she told you, that we don't care for her?" he asked.

I nodded, because I couldn't get the words out.

"Martha is a very sick girl," he said, his shoulders sagging. "We brought her home because we thought she was improving. . . ."

I thought about leukemia and heart disease.

"What's wrong with Joy?" I asked.

I wasn't sure if he was trying to evade the question when he said, "Why do you keep calling her Joy?"

"That's what she called herself. Isn't it her nickname or something?"

"No. Her only name is Martha."

"Then what's wrong with *Martha*?"

"She has . . . emotional problems."

I remembered Joy saying, "They'll stop at nothing to get me back. They'll tell lies."

"Emotional problems?" I said. "She always got A's in class."

"Emotional problems have nothing to do with intelligence," he said.

"She told me you'll do anything to keep her from her boyfriend."

"Gilbert Gabhart," he said quietly.

"Yes, Gil Gabhart. They're in love. Why can't you let them be happy?"

He sank back in his chair. "Gil Gabhart is Martha's psychiatrist."

"No." I shook my head. "I don't believe that. It's a lie."

He sank back in his chair. "What have I ever lied to you about?"

"Joy said you were Jewish."

He looked perplexed. "We're Episcopalian."

"She told me that Old Mr. Glass can talk if he wants to."

Mr. Glass looked at his father for a few seconds, then said, "My father hasn't been able to speak since his stroke four years ago."

The Flanders School. Emotional problems. Joy. Martha. The thoughts pelted down like rain.

186

"Why don't you tell me your story," he said, and indicated the seat in front of his desk. We faced each other, and I told him the whole truth, no lies. I told him how I'd gone in the chapel where I shouldn't have been; I told him about meeting Joy in the woods. I told him Joy's plan. I told him about the money. I even told him what Joy had said about Mrs. Glass and where she went on weekends.

When I finished, he looked very angry. Again he reminded me of my father. He stared at me long and hard. Finally he said, "My wife used to drive down to Boston to visit Martha at the Flanders School. Every other weekend."

It made sense.

And somehow, when he said that, I knew it was all over. As hard as I tried, I couldn't hide from the truth: Joy was the liar.

Mr. Glass leaned forward. "And now let me tell you the other half of the story," he said. "This is the story of a privileged fifteen-year-old boy who was mad at the world."

I jumped up. "I'm not mad at *anything*!" But the violence in my voice denied the words even as I spoke.

He continued: "A boy who didn't want to be here—"

"I did too!"

"—at Grey Oaks. A boy who was trying to find a way to vent his anger against his father and his name and found a perfect act of rebellion that was sure to get him expelled. Again."

Tears in my eyes distorted the shape of Mr. Glass behind his desk. "Am I?" I whispered. "Expelled?"

He nodded, then got up and left the room.

I turned to Old Mr. Glass and said, "Can you understand why I did it? Wouldn't you have done the same thing? If you were me? If you met a girl like Joy—someone who just wanted to be happy?" But he didn't even look at me. What was the point, talking to him? It was about as useless as screaming into the wind.

On my last night at Grey Oaks I stood in the doorway of my room. I wanted to trash it. I wanted to tear the bookshelves from the wall and empty the wastebasket on the floor. I wanted to rip up the carpet and break all the windows. Instead I packed my bags.

When Stephen came in, my bags were stacked at the foot of the bed, but he didn't notice. I wanted to strangle him. He was in a pretty good mood, as he'd just come back from visiting Katie.

"Katie says you're mad at the world," he said conversationally. "She says you're mad at your dad for putting you in Grey Oaks and you're mad at the school. Katie says that helping Joy was your way of getting rid of hostile feelings. She says—"

"Katie says, Katie says, Katie says!" I shouted. All

day people had been telling me how angry I was. Now I felt like the top of my head was going to explode. "Does she tell you I'm kicked out of this place? The only place that ever felt like home? Maybe now that I'm leaving, Katie Says can move in here with you—but you'd probably be too sick to make it with her anyway."

Stephen banged out of the room, and I went into the john with every intention of dumping all of his medications right down the sink. But I couldn't do that to him. Instead I knocked the Dixie dispenser off the wall with my fist, sending the paper cups scattering across the floor. I opened my mouth but not a sound came out.

That night I had a nightmare. Dark, empty faces swooped down at me, screaming and crying like babies, sometimes calling out loud for their mothers. Then a pale light appeared, and for the first time a face wasn't empty. I could see the features, and it was Joy. I could hear myself screaming as another head began to turn around. I woke up right before I saw the face, but I knew it would be my own.

Stephen was shaking my shoulder. "I'm not waking you because I feel sorry for you," he said. "I'm only doing it because I don't want you waking all the other guys."

But he brought me a glass of water. I remembered the Dixie cups scattered all over the bathroom floor;

I also remembered that this was the glass he kept his toothbrush in. My hand was shaking so hard I spilled half the water on the bed.

"Thanks," I said.

"I'm not talking to you." He climbed into his bunk.

I couldn't stand it when someone was mad at me. I remembered a night two years ago when my father was mad because of a bad report card. We argued all the way to the airport, and when it came time to get on the plane, he refused to sit next to me. There was a terrible thunderstorm that night, and I ended up gripping the arms of my seat while my father sat twelve rows back. It was one of the worst nights of my life. I poked the bottom of Stephen's bunk with my foot. "I'm sorry about the things I said earlier."

"No, you're not."

"Yeah, I am." I placed the empty glass on the windowsill and stared through it at the moon and stars, which now looked blurred and distorted.

After a moment he said, "They're really kicking you out?"

I told him everything Mr. Glass had said, but it was hard. For one thing my nightmare kept getting mixed up with the story. In the past the nightmares faded fast; now that my dreams had faces, I didn't know if I'd ever forget. When I finished, neither of us said anything for a long time. I thought he had fallen asleep, but then his voice came through the darkness: "Expelled! Doesn't that piss the hell out of you?"

The next morning he sat on the bunk in his jockey shorts, with his left foot pulled way up in front of his face, one hand holding the foot, the other holding *Taber's Medical Dictionary.* "I think I've got a plantar wart," he said. Same shorts, same dictionary, same foot as on the first day I met him. Different disease. "See ya, Henry," he said, shaking my hand.

Mr. Glass escorted me downstairs, and all along the hallway I saw faces framed in doorways, staring at me. A couple of the guys said, "Bye," but most of them only stared. I remembered Joy saying, "Do you know what it's like to leave everyone and everything you love?" I knew I'd remember the brown-and-gray walls for the rest of my life.

Then we were outside. All the leaves had blown off the trees during the night, and the sidewalk looked as if it were covered with a wet red-and-yellow carpet. I passed the maple tree—now bare—for the last time. Beyond the gate was the familiar black limousine, and tears sprang into my eyes because I knew the only one in it would be the chauffeur.

Without a word Mr. Glass unlatched the gate, and I was no longer a part of Grey Oaks. The pounding in my head got louder, and a bird swooped down at me like a face in my dreams.

191

I was mad.

Mad at Joy, mad at my father, mad at the school. Mad at the guys. Mad at the world. Why had I done it? Hadn't I known it would end like this? Did I really *want* to leave here?

"*An act of rebellion . . .*" "*A way to vent your anger . . .*" "*Katie says you're mad . . .*"

The words rolled around in my skull like marbles. I was screaming as I walked toward the car, bellowing out my rage—screaming without a wind to absorb it. Screaming because I had to leave, screaming at them for maybe being right all along.

A month later I was flying to a new boarding school on my dad's company jet. He was in Los Angeles. For five weeks I'd been privately tutored while my father's secretary, Elena, made inquiries at boarding schools all over the country. This time I was on my way to Saint Croix Academy in Oregon. I reached into my travel bag for the letter Elena had handed me as I boarded the plane. It was from Stephen Hall.

Henry:

This is your old roommate Stephen writing. I'm sending this in care of your father's company because I don't know where you live, and the school won't tell me. You're sort of persona non grata around here. I've already got a new roommate— a scholarship student from Ohio who hacks and coughs all night long. He's either got an advanced case of TB or walking pneumonia. He won't even go for a chest X ray! My own health is iffy. Right now I'm experiencing some tightness in the forehead, so the doctor is sending me for a CAT scan. It doesn't look good.

But the real reason I'm writing is this: Martha Glass, aka "Joy," is back in the news. Last week they told us to "notify Mr. Glass if you see his daughter anywhere around the premises." Turns out she escaped from the asylum! Katie says that before Joy left the nuthouse, she was telling some of the doctors there about how she was in love with this wonderful rich boy from Grey Oaks named Henry who wanted to <u>marry</u> her! So don't be surprised if somewhere, someway, somehow, when you least expect it, that crazy chick ends up on your doorstep. But where is your doorstep anyway?

I turned away from the letter and looked out the window. Beneath the thin layer of clouds, a million houses were below me. A million houses, a million doorsteps. *"Where is your doorstep anyway?"*

I didn't know.

Walking

Man, everybody in that school was famous for something. Laurie Brogan was famous for all A's. Borden Kosh was the football captain. Anna Marie Naylor had the biggest chest. But I was famous for walking out. It's not as good as being football captain, but when you're five foot three like me, you better know they don't ask you to join the football squad. Screw it. I wouldn't want to play football anyway.

So like I said, I was famous for walking out of that school—just getting up and *walking*, right in the middle of an English class or something. At first it was some big deal, but later on nobody even cared—or maybe they'd say, "There he goes again," when I'd get up during some social-sciences test or something, but the teachers didn't chase after me in the hall no more. They didn't chase after me, screaming, "Jackie, you get back here," like Mrs. Duke done the first time I walked out. By the way, my name may be Jackie, but I'm no girl. I'm not like a Jacqueline or something. I'm just a guy named Jackie, and that's what it says on the birth certificate.

Anyway, I want to tell you about this one time I walked out. It was a Monday—a real springtime type of day—all the windows open, so you could hear somebody mowing the lawn, and the bells from the Good Humor truck. And it smelled really good—the flowers outside and the lawn. Who wants to be in school on a day like that? *Everybody* in that class would of liked to walk out—the most famous chest and the most famous football captain, and even Mrs. Fergus, the teacher. You could tell because she gave us some dumb essay on "My Most Amusing Friend" so she could just sit there at her desk and file her nails.

But I guess I was about the only one who had the guts to *really* get up and do it.

Nobody cared or noticed. Only reason *I* noticed is 'cause you gotta pay attention to yourself when your feet are moving.

Out. That was about the only thought in my mind. Out. Behind me some girl with a thin face and hot-shot hall-monitor armband was saying, "Do you have a pass?" But I kept walking. Just turned off my ears and let my feet do my talking. Walking.

When I got out, first place I went was looking for that Good Humor truck. No luck. Then I remembered what my dad always says about me eating candy and ice cream: Don't. I'm not supposed to eat them 'cause they make me hyper. My dad likes me to eat fruit instead. That's okay, because I like apples and stuff too.

I just wish they sold apples off a truck like ice cream. The problem with apples is you got to go someplace special to buy them. You can't get them from a 7–Eleven or down at the Beer-and-Wine. About the only place I know to get fruit is grocery stores, and I hate grocery stores. Everybody always follows you around, just 'cause you're a kid. They think you're gonna steal. A long time ago my dad said, "I ever catch you stealing, I'll bust your ass." He would, too. I remember one time I went up to the grocery to buy some cream-of-mushroom soup for my dad's dinner. Man, they followed me from aisle A to aisle K. The guy who followed me carried a box of spaghetti in one hand and pretended to be just some other shopper, but he didn't have a coat on and it was like January or something. I mean, is anybody that dumb? So while this guy's following me, who do I see but this girl from my typing class, Lydia McIntyre. Well, she's pushing a shopping cart, and walking like she always does, like she's trying to touch her forehead with her nose. Nobody gives her Look Number Two, even though in our school she's most famous for being a klepto.

Just thinking about that grocery store made me mad, so my feet kept walking right past it. Before I knew it, I was on Warren Avenue, which is up by my house. But instead of walking home, I went the other direction, over the Southfield Expressway. Warren's not bad, if you compare it to a lot of streets in Detroit. The part I was walking on has lots of dentists' offices and business places and even a fortune-teller called Mrs. Reader. But there's also a fruit-and-vegetable store up there. I didn't think the store even had a name, 'cause all the sign said was FRUITS, VEGETABLES. Later on I found out that's the name of the store: Fruits, Vegetables. I don't think that's a very good name for a store. Especially since they sell some other stuff, like milk and eggs and salami.

Outside the store was a big table filled with grapes and watermelons and cans of tuna fish. I don't know why the tuna was out there either. A fat man in a purple apron was standing in the doorway, reading a book with a map on the cover. I don't trust people who read a lot. I squeezed past the man, and I really mean squeezed. 'Cause as little as I am, his stomach was so big it almost touched mine. And it wasn't just a beer belly like my dad. I'm talking fat face and arms and legs and fingers. Probably toes too, if you could see them.

"Good morning," he said. "Or is it afternoon now?"

It was afternoon, but I just lifted my shoulders like I didn't know. I don't like people asking me questions.

The apples didn't look too good, so it took me a

long time to pick a couple out. While I was picking through them, a kid about my age or maybe older came through a swinging metal door in the back of the store. He was wearing a purple apron too. The kid's face was so shiny you'd think his nose would slide right off it. Then there was his hair, and, man, he never stopped fooling with it. You know: combing it, pushing it down, pulling it back. I didn't think he should be doing that around so much food.

"Hey, Pop," he said. "I'm going over to take a look at Davy's new car."

"Oh, no, you don't," said the fat man, putting down his book.

Both of them talked funny, like maybe they wasn't born here. I pretended I was looking at grapefruit, 'cause it sounded like they was getting ready to fight and I like to watch fights.

"You *said* I could go over to see that car," said the kid.

"I said you could do it after you cleaned out the walk-in. You done that yet?" The fat man started to get kind of sweaty, like he knew they was gonna fight.

"Can't I come back tonight and clean the walk-in?" said the kid, almost like he might back down.

"Who's going to open the store for you tonight? I've got classes tonight." Classes! I couldn't believe it. The man must of been forty or fifty years old.

"Then I'll do it tomorrow," said the kid.

"And who's going to work the cash register while

you're in back cleaning? I'll be at my citizenship class."

"You and your classes," said the kid.

I was glad he said that, 'cause I felt like saying it too.

The kid said, "We wouldn't have these kind of problems if you'd hire somebody else to work here, you know."

I thought his dad would belt him one, but he didn't. He just nodded his head and said, "I know. I've got to put up another help wanted sign."

You know what I thought about? I thought about all the times my teachers said if I didn't pay attention and learn something, I'd never get a job. And this sounded like a job. I wondered if I'd still have to go to school if I had a job.

I said, "You need somebody to work here, mister?"

He said, "You know somebody who needs a job?"

I said, "Yeah, me."

The kid busted out laughing. "You? What are you, kid, ten years old?"

People think just 'cause your size is little, your age is little too. I hate that. I told him I was in high school, and he started laughing even harder. Around here we can't get into school if we're not wearing our picture ID clipped on our collar or belt. Lucky I still had mine on, because he didn't believe me until I showed him the Cody High School ID.

It's funny, but I thought I liked that kid until he started all that laughing. Then I liked his father better. His father said, "Have you ever worked in a store?"

"I sold things before," I said, which is really true, 'cause once a month my dad and me rent a booth at the flea market and sell stuff we make.

"What kind of grades do you get in school?" he asked, and you could tell grades in school would mean a lot to a man that old who still took classes.

I said, "Mostly B's and C's." I didn't say what classes I got those grades in. If he wanted to think I got B's in Advanced Computerized Chemical Biology, that was his problem. Because really I take all the R classes: R. reading, R. math and R. study skills. That's what it says right on my schedule, and one day Ricky Lenz told me the R stands for retarded. But somebody else said, "Shut up, Ricky. It means remedial." I asked this old lady who taught me English what "remedial" meant, and she said, "Needs improvement."

That didn't sound so bad compared to retarded.

But I guess you're thinking I should of told him they was remedial classes. Maybe I should of. But I don't like to put myself down. That's not stuck-up, that's just being good to yourself.

'Cause, man, it seemed like *somebody* was always putting me down. For not being smart enough, or tall enough, or 'cause my hair is so short and red that I look like a battery all rusted out on top. Kids, and sometimes teachers, called me

"Red" or "Peewee" or "Shorty." One time a teacher back in middle school even called me a dummy.

I hate when people call me a dummy.

Because I'm not a dummy. I just can't sit still.

I guess that's why I don't put myself down. 'Cause other people do it so much.

The fat man told me he'd pay me three fifty an hour and that I should start right then. He said he'd find an apron for me.

The kid said, "Ho, ho, ho. Why don't you just tie a dust cloth around him, Pop? That would probably fit him all right."

His father didn't like that, 'cause he said, "Junior, I don't want to hear you talking that way to Jackie again."

He found an apron, but I didn't feel like a sissy for wearing it 'cause both the man and his son was wearing them. He had to fold it up a couple times before he tied it around my butt. Then he shook my hand and said, "Welcome to Fruits, Vegetables." He told me his name, but I didn't get it. It sounded like Larry Puckaholic. When I tried to say that name, he just said, "Call me Larry."

Nobody ever did tell me the kid's name, but everybody called him Junior—even some of the customers—so I guess that was it.

My first job was to clean out that walk-in. Turns out a walk-in is a giant refrigerator filled with fruits and vegetables. It was in back of those metal doors in a place called the stockroom. Junior was supposed to help me, but he just sat on the sink back there and bitched. "It ain't fair he's paying you three fifty and I'm only making three seventy-five," he said.

I thought it was pretty fair, considering he wasn't doing nothing and I was working my butt off. First I took all the fruits and vegetables out of the freezer and piled them on big tables. Some of the fruit was loose, and some was in heavy boxes. It took a long time to get all that out. When the big metal shelves was all empty, I took them out of the walk-in. They weren't too heavy, but they was so cruddy they looked like they had a skin disease. Finally I took out these wooden boards that covered the floor. They were pretty big squares, all slatted.

Junior didn't seem too happy about the way I was working. He asked me did I want to go out in the alley and smoke a joint. When I told him I don't touch that shit, he looked like he didn't believe me and went out there by his self.

I had to scrub and scrub the walk-in floor with a metal brush, but I could of used a blowtorch. But you know what? After I finished that floor and washed down the walls, it was shiny and I felt pretty good about it. I like to clean. I don't know why. Maybe it's 'cause me and my dad clean our house every Sunday, and he used to be in the Navy and the Navy likes things really clean.

I scraped those wooden squares, then put them back on the floor. After I cleaned the metal racks and

put them in the walk-in, I loaded the fruits and vegetables inside.

When Larry saw the walk-in, he said, "Holy
cow!"

I said, "Is that okay?"

"I never saw it so clean!" said Larry.

Junior said, "I showed him how to do it."

"Don't give me that!" said Larry. "Your idea of
cleaning is to sponge off any part of the wall that
doesn't have a rack in front of it."

"Are you saying this red-headed shrimp does a
better job than *me*?" said Junior, just like he couldn't
believe it.

Larry smacked Junior across the back of the head
a couple times, talking some kind of foreign. It
sounded like "Yicketa-yacketa, yee-yee-yee."

That night I told my dad I got a job. We was
playing cards when I told him. We do that a lot.
We're the only people I know without a TV. He says
there's enough killing going on here in Detroit without watching it three or four hours a night.

Mostly we make things downstairs in his work-
shop. Duck decoys, stools, and bookshelves to sell
at the flea market. Or we play table hockey or cards.
He also tells me about some of the stuff he reads in
the paper and—this is the worst part—every night I
got to read him an article from the *Reader's Digest*
'cause he says by that time of day his eyes get tired.
Man, it takes forever to read that damn thing. And

I got to read every word, no skipping, and if I don't know how to say the word right, I got to look it up in the dictionary. My most unforgettable article was one that took two hours and seventeen minutes to read, 'cause it was over five pages. But did my dad say one word about that? Nope, not one. He just sat there with his eyes shut, listening, for two hours and seventeen minutes and didn't say a word.

That night I could tell he was just getting ready to ask me to read from the *Digest*. I thought I could hold him off for a while by telling him about Fruits, Vegetables. That's what I thought! But he said, "Tell me about this job . . . right after you read me an article from the *Digest*." Damn, that made me mad, but I guess I never read an article faster than I did that night, 'cause I really wanted to tell him about Larry and Junior and how I had my own apron.

After I told him, he said, "Now, make sure this job doesn't interfere with school."

I didn't have the guts to tell him I thought I might not have to go to school no more when I had a job.

"How much money do you expect to bring home from that market?" he asked, pulling out a toothpick.

I said, "Three fifty an hour, and I work three hours on school days and six hours on Saturday. That makes . . ." He waited till I figured that and didn't help me out. He never does.

When I told him how much, he said, "Every week I want you to take ten dollars and put it in the fishbowl."

"Why?"

He said, " 'Cause I said so."

When he says that, you don't argue.

The fishbowl is where we put money ever since my goldfish, Evie, died. Every night he puts his loose change in it, and every Friday he puts in one ten, one five and five singles. All the flea-market money goes in it. We use that money for school lunches and bus rides and seats at Tiger games. I guess it's fair I should put something in it, even though I didn't want to, 'cause it's for the family.

In case you're wondering where my mother fits into all this, she don't. When people ask me where she is, I tell them she lives in Tahiti. And who knows, maybe she might. She left when I was three, and we ain't seen her since. But we get along okay without her, my dad and me, and you know why? 'Cause my dad really, really likes me. He yells at me a lot, and sometimes hits me, but even then there's this something—I don't know what you call it—but even then you can tell he really, really likes me. And I don't think it would matter *what* I did in this world, it wouldn't stop him from liking me. I don't understand it.

I was glad he didn't mind I had a job. And I was glad to be back at Fruits, Vegetables the next day too, until I found out Larry was going off for a class and leaving Junior in charge.

Junior worked at the cash register, and I was supposed to sweep the floor and bring in stock—that's

what they call all the stuff at Fruits, Vegetables—
whenever things ran low. Junior kept dropping stuff
on the floor when I swept, but I kept sweeping and
didn't say nothing about it. He told me he hoped his
girlfriend wasn't pregnant and asked me did I have
one. I told him "Sure," but I was lying. I like girls but
don't know one who likes me back.

Then Junior told me to bring a cart of cabbage
from the walk-in. "You got a lot of cabbage on the
shelf now," I said.

"Get more cabbage and that's an order," he said.

So I filled up a shopping cart with cabbages, but
as soon as I brought it out, he told me he changed
his mind and I should put it all away again. Then he
said to bring out some boxes of strawberries. I carried them out, and he said, "Idiot! Go put them
back. You should have seen we've already got ten
pints in that bin!"

I figured out what was going on.

When he told me to bring out some cartons of
eggs, I didn't know if I should tell him to shove it or
if I should just walk. That's what I felt like doing.

But then I looked over at the refrigerator section
and saw that we really was low on eggs.

Since there wasn't any customers in the store, he
followed me out to the stockroom. There's a little
door on the side of the walk-in where you can pull
out one crate of eggs at a time. Junior leaned over
and watched me rip open a crate of eggs and take

out the cartons, but he didn't help me none. After about two minutes, he opened one of the small cartons and said, "Like eggs?" and I thought, Uh-oh. 'Cause that's just not the kind of question one guy asks another one unless he's planning something.

Sure enough, an egg came flying at me. "Think fast, Red."

I caught it.

I'm quick.

Besides, I was sort of expecting it.

But I wasn't expecting two, three, four, five, *six* eggs zooming across the room. Flying eggs is kind of funny—like birds that ain't hatched yet trying to fly. But it ain't so funny when you're trying to catch the damn things. I caught the second egg, but when I caught the third egg, I dropped Egg Number One.

Egg Number Four, Number Five, and Number Six all splat too.

I looked down at my shoes, and they was all covered with slimy clear-and-yellow stuff. Looked like an elephant sneezed on them, and they sort of squished when I walked out the door of the stockroom, right through the store. Screw it, I thought, I didn't want to work here anyway. I was just going out the door when I banged right into old Larry coming back from his class. He said, "Are you taking your break now?"

Nobody ever said I got a break, so I just made a face and lifted my shoulders.

I wanted to walk around him, but he was too big. It was the first time anybody ever stopped me from leaving someplace.

He leaned down so close to me that I could see little hairs growing out of his face in places where I didn't know you could grow hair. "Is Junior making trouble?" he asked.

I didn't want Junior to think he won over me, so I said, "No!" I was lying. I think Larry knew I was lying, 'cause he turned me around and walked back to the stockroom with one arm around my shoulder. Junior was cleaning up the eggs from the floor. "What happened here?" said Larry.

Junior said to me, "I thought you were leaving, Shrimp."

Larry said, "Never you mind, Junior. What are you cleaning from that floor?"

Junior said, "I dropped some eggs."

He made a mistake saying that, 'cause Larry said, "Why were you back here dropping eggs when working the stockroom was Jackie's job today?"

Junior's face got even shinier, like it was about to bust. "Well, I'll tell you, Pop." He waited like he was trying to think of a good one. "I'll tell you. I told the kid we needed more eggs, and he told me to go to hell, he didn't want to get them. So I came back here to get 'em myself, and I thought I heard somebody out front fooling around with the cash register. I was rushing so I could catch him in the act, and that's when I dropped the eggs."

208

That was the biggest lie I ever heard in my life. My feet turned around and pointed toward the door, but before I could take Step One, Larry's over there beating the side of Junior's head saying, "Yicketa-yacketa, yee-yee-yee." Then he made Junior shake my hand and say, "I'm sorry, man." But you know what? I didn't believe Junior for one second there. He squeezed my hand so tight that the bones inside squeaked against each other, and he whispered, "I'm gonna get you for this."

From then on Larry was especially nice to me. The next day he made Junior work in the stockroom, and he showed me how to use the cash register. First time I rang up a sale, it came to $7037.43. The lady customer about had a heart attack, but Larry helped me figure out the problem. Junior said I was so damn slow at the cash register that the customer's eggs and milk got spoiled while they was still standing in line. I was slow, but after a while I never made mistakes. One time a customer who looked like my very worst schoolteacher kept making noises like spit was filling up her throat—all because I wasn't fast. She said, "I don't know what's taking so long, young man. The total should be three dollars and eighty cents." But you know what? She was wrong! It should of been three dollars and ninety-five cents, 'cause she forgot to add sales tax. Like I said, I was slow, but I never made mistakes.

Something else happened too, but not at the store. A whole week went by without me walking out of school. I thought they should of put me in the *Guinness Book* for that. The reason I wasn't walking was this: One day I was in my R. math class and my feet was getting that itching feeling again. Suddenly I heard the teacher telling how important it was to add long rows of numbers like $28 + 93 + 17 + 46 + 104 + 59$, and I thought, That's what I do at the store! I add up long rows of numbers! I almost raised my hand and told the teacher about it, but I didn't. But I did get an A on my workbook page that day.

Then in R. social sciences we was supposed to be reading about South America when all of a sudden the teacher said the word bananas. Well, I knew a lot about bananas by then. How to tell when they're ripe and when they're old. How you should store them. How much we charged a pound. When we took a social-sciences test, I still got a D, but I did get all the questions about bananas right.

I guess I felt better about school knowing Larry still had to go a lot. He took citizenship classes on Tuesday afternoons, and night-school classes on Monday and Wednesday. I thought about what it was like to have your own store, and I thought about how maybe I should get my own store someday. Not fruits and vegetables, but maybe selling stuff like my dad and me build. I could even get my dad to work for me, 'cause right now he works in a factory and one time a machine took a hunk out of his thumb.

One Tuesday, I was working the cash register and

Junior was cleaning the walk-in. "Make sure to do it as good as Jackie," said Larry.

Junior gave his father the finger behind his back.

Larry took off his apron and got his schoolbooks out. "I'm leaving now," he said. "Keep your eye on the store, Jackie."

I couldn't believe it, 'cause that's what he always said to Junior when he left. He never said that to me before.

Junior said, "I'll take care of things around here, Pop."

Larry said, "You go clean that walk-in. Jackie's in charge today."

It was the first time I was ever in charge of anything.

Man, I walked around that store like my chest was full of air. There was lots of customers, and I always said, "Yes, ma'am!" and "Yes, sir!" and "Please come back again!" just like Larry done.

A little while later Junior came running out of the stockroom, breathing hard. "Quick, Jackie! The walk-in's busted!"

Even though we had four ladies shopping over by the beets and cabbages, I left the cash register and went into the stockroom.

It was real quiet back there 'cause the walk-in wasn't humming like usual.

"What are we gonna do? What are we gonna do?" said Junior. "All the stock is gonna rot, and Pop will fire you."

Just from the way he wasn't looking me in the face, I knew that walk-in didn't turn itself off. I knew he done it just to get me in trouble. I just walked to the side of that big refrigerator and pushed the off-on switch, and it started humming.

He said, "Oh, you're real smart. A real Einstein."

I didn't know what Einstein was, but I said, "I ain't all that smart, but I ain't all that dumb, either."

But he wasn't done with me yet. A couple minutes later he came running out and said, "Jackie, come quick! There's some kind of oil leaking inside the walk-in."

Since there was only one man back in the oranges section, I followed Junior to the stockroom. I knew it would be a trick. He opened the door of the walk-in and said, "See back there? Running down that wall?" There really was something on the wall, so I went in to look. It was only tomato slime. But while I was standing there, I heard the big metal door slam shut on me.

That's usually no big deal, 'cause it opens from the inside, but I could hear Junior dragging something over—probably one of the big tables—and pushing it up against the door. Sure enough, when I tried to open the door, it wouldn't even budge.

It was dark in there 'cause the light only comes on when the door's open—just like the refrigerator at home. It was *cold* in there too.

I sat down on a watermelon to think.

Junior was probably up at the cash register right now, overcharging the customers and acting like a hotshot. He always messed with his hair when he was bagging orders. He was not a good worker. Not like I was. I remember the time he packed a gallon of milk on top of a carton of eggs, and this lady came back to the store 'cause nine of the eggs was busted.

Eggs!

I had the idea of my lifetime at that second. I thought about how you didn't have to open the big door at the back of the walk-in to get eggs. Somewhere behind all those boxes, way over on the right side, was the little door where you could pull out one crate at a time. That little door was little, but so was I.

I pulled crates around in the dark until I found the little door, pushed it open, and slid right out. When I got back to the front of the store, Junior was weighing grapefruits for somebody and combing his hair. When he saw me, his mouth opened so wide I could of popped one of those grapefruits into it whole.

I took the fruit out of his hands and started weighing it. "Thanks for helping out with this customer," I said. "I'll call if I need you for anything else."

I thought that was a pretty funny thing to say.

He walked back to the stockroom with his mouth still hanging open.

So by then I was really getting into this being-in-charge stuff.

About a half hour later the door opened and in walked Lydia McIntyre, that girl from my school most famous for being a klepto.

She was the only customer in the store right then, so there was lots of time to watch her moving around, pretending to look at peaches and grapes.

Sure enough, when she walked past the apple bin, she picked up an apple, then pretended to scratch her leg. The apple disappeared.

"Hey, Lydia!" I said.

She looked surprised that I knew her name. I never talk to her. I don't talk to any of them in my class, even though I know all their names and know a lot of stuff about them. I said, "You better pay for that apple in your pocket."

"Apple? What are you talking about?"

"I'm talking about that apple you took and didn't pay for."

"How dare you! I ought to call the manager," she said. "Who's in charge?"

"I am."

You know what it felt like to say that? It was the best feeling I ever had in my life. It felt so good that I had to say it again: "I am."

She started swinging her neck from side to side with her lips pushed together. "No way!" she said.

But I just kept walking up to her with my right hand reaching out, ready for her to give that apple to me. The funny thing was: The closer I walked to her, the more she backed away. And she didn't stop until she banged into the cantaloupe display. "Now look what you did," she said, as the cantaloupes rolled off the counter. Man, thirty of them must of fallen onto the floor.

But I just stood there, holding out my hand, saying to Lydia, "Give me back that apple."

She looked to the left and she looked to the right. I didn't know what she was looking for, but whatever it was, she wasn't finding it. Then she jerked this apple out of her pocket and *slammed* it into my hand. I remembered how Larry said to always be polite, so I said, "Thank you," but she didn't want to hear that. She just pushed past me and went running out the door.

Man!

I thought I couldn't feel any better if I won a hundred million dollars in the Lotto or got engaged to a movie star. Right at that minute it felt like I could do anything in the world.

Then Junior came out from the stockroom.

My good mood squashed like one of them cantaloupes on the floor.

"So it's just you and me here," he said.

I tried to make my voice sound regular. "We had a customer, but she left."

"You're leaving too," he said. He put his arms up and wrapped his big fingers around the top edge of the doorway. I couldn't believe anyone could be so huge. "Get out of here or I'll take you out of here in pieces," he said.

215

So that was that. He wasn't screwing around no more, and he meant what he was saying. Those big muscles was sort of rolling around inside his arms. It didn't matter who was the best worker, or who was smarter or nicer to the customers. What mattered was that he was big and I wasn't. That's all that mattered.

I turned toward the door. I wondered what Larry would say when he found out I was gone. I guessed he wouldn't trust me in charge of the store no more. I guessed I wouldn't even be working at the store no more. My feet hadn't took a step yet, but inside myself, I was walking. Hell, I was *running*! But I wasn't sure where I was running to. Or what I'd do when I got there. When I figured that part out, I'd walk. Maybe. But not until then.

I looked at Junior and picked up a cantaloupe. He looked at me. I put the cantaloupe into the bin. He kept looking at me. When a couple of seconds went by and I still wasn't dead, I turned my back on him and started piling those cantaloupes one on top of another. Finally he swore real loud, and I heard the stockroom door slam. I turned around and saw he was gone. I felt so good for a minute there that I juggled a couple cantaloupes. You know why? 'Cause I was still alive, and my feet was standing still.

SC
SIE

Sieruta, Peter D.

Heartbeats and
other stories

$12.89